I decided to skim the JAM column. IGNORED wants to know how to get the boy in math class to notice her again. Loser league. PUNISHED doesn't know how to convince her parents her curfew is unreasonable. My advice in three words? *Talk to them*.

"Read one out loud," Ringo said.

"Okay, here's one from I KNOW HE CARES. Probably some quivering mouse who eats heart-shaped cereal for breakfast." Holding back a snicker, I read on:

> "Sometimes someone I really love gets mad when I mess things up. He doesn't understand that I can't help it. When I screw up, he goes wild. He hits me. Sometimes it's really bad. It's hard to hide the bruises."

Ringo just stared at his drawing. Silently, I reread the letter. This wasn't the sniveling complaint of a loser. This kid was hurting.

Big time.

SERIES

GET REAL #1:
Girl Reporter Blows Lid off Town!

GET REAL #2:
Girl Reporter Sinks School!

GET REAL #3:
Girl Reporter Stuck in Jam!

Coming soon:
GET REAL #4:
Girl Reporter Snags Crush!

Girl Reporter Stuck in Jam!

Created by
LINDA ELLERBEE

AVON BOOKS ■ NEW YORK

A Division of HarperCollins*Publishers*

My deepest thanks to Katherine Drew,
Anne-Marie Cunniffe, Lori Seidner, Whitney Malone,
Roz Noonan, Alix Reid and Susan Katz, without whom
this series of books would not exist. I also want to thank
Christopher Hart, whose book *Drawing on the Funny
Side of the Brain* retaught me how to cartoon. At
age 11, I was better at it than I am now. Honest.

Drawings by Linda Ellerbee

AVON BOOKS TRADEMARK REG. U.S. PAT. OFF.
AND IN OTHER COUNTRIES, MARCA REGISTRADA, HECHO EN U.S.A.

Girl Reporter Stuck in Jam!
Copyright © 2000 by Lucky Duck Productions, Inc.
Produced by By George Productions, Inc.

Library of Congress Cataloging-in-Publication Data
Ellerbee, Linda.
    Girl reporter stuck in jam! / created by Linda Ellerbee.
        p.   cm. — (Get real ; #3)
    Summary: Intrepid eleven-year-old journalist Casey Smith is so busy
trying to get a story for the newspaper about a victim of physical abuse
that she neglects her friend Ringo, the school's first male cheerleader.
    ISBN 0-06-440757-8 (pbk.) — ISBN 0-06-028247-9 (lib. bdg.)
    [1. Child abuse—Fiction.   2. Journalism—Fiction.   3. Newspapers—
Fiction.   4. Schools—Fiction.   5. Cheerleading—Fiction.   6. Sex role—
Fiction.]   I. Title.   II. Series: Ellerbee, Linda. Get real ; #3.
PZ7.E42845Gj   2000   99-40605
[Fic]—dc21   CIP
                                                                      AC

Typography by Carla Weise
1   2   3   4   5   6   7   8   9   10
❖
First Edition

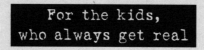
For the kids,
who always get real

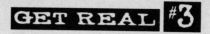

Girl Reporter
Stuck in Jam!

Girl Reporter Vanishes

MY NAME IS Casey Smith, and I'm invisible.

I kid you not. I can walk down the corridors of Trumbull Middle School without being seen or heard.

Maybe it's my disguise. Brown hair. Brown eyes. Brown freckles.

Jeans. T-shirt. Sneakers. I'll admit, high fashion is not exactly up there on my list of World Issues to Explore. My idea of dressing up is deciding which of my eight pairs of Converse hightops to put on. Today I went with the brown theme.

It's not just clothing that makes me invisible. It's my *life*. I'm an eleven-year-old journalist stuck in the hopelessly small town of Abbington in the not-so-majestic Berkshire Mountains of western Massachusetts. At the moment I was holed up

1

in my power center—the newsroom of Trumbull Middle School.

Don't let the gray walls and scarred old desks and polka-dotted lime-green table fool you. Important stuff happens here.

Like the e-mail I was writing to my best friend, Griffin Kenny. He moved away last year, but through the magic of computers, I keep bugging him.

To: Thebeast
From: Wordpainter

Something is seriously wrong. I'm invisible. At least I'm *becoming* invisible. Right now I'm watching my fingers fade from the keyboard. I'm vanishing as I write!

The thing is, if a reporter writes a story in a small town and no one is there to read it, does the story make a sound?

Because I've been coming up with some megaton stories . . . with zero impact.

At least, not the big prize: the Pulitzer. Yup, the big banana of journalism prizes. The Oscar of scribbling. The . . . oh, forget it.

Write Back Soon, Casey

I'll admit I was being melodramatic. But just a little. After all, I had blown the lid off Trumbull with major front-page stories: toxic waste, cheating conspiracies. Stories that grabbed the reader and didn't let go. I don't think I'm bragging when I say that I was personally responsible for bringing real news to our school paper, *Real News*.

So why hadn't the prize patrol called? Why did that voice in my head keep saying: "*You?* You think *you* can write? Get over yourself!"

Not that I would ever mention that voice to any of the other *Real News* staffers. Certainly not to Megan O'Connor, Our Totally Perky Editor. She'd probably stage a group hug or send me a "cheer-up" note with happy flowers dancing in the margins.

But I could say anything to Griffin. He was my best friend, even though he now lived a zillion miles away from Abbington. I clicked the icon to send my e-mail. Then I looked at the material I had downloaded from the Internet.

Pulitzer Prize–winning stories.

They were the reason I was sitting in the newspaper office on a Friday after school. I figured if I wanted to win a prize, I needed to study past winners. Besides, I had time to kill before I hooked up with Ringo, my geographically friendly best friend.

Hmm. One journalist had won for "comprehensive coverage of a botched bank robbery and police shoot-out." Another for a "compassionate narrative portrait of a mother and two daughters slain on a Florida vacation." There were awards for reporting on "the chaos and devastation" following an earthquake. . . .

Now *that* was news. Exactly the kind of meaty stuff I wanted to cover. And not just to win a prize. I like to get answers. Kids need to know what's really going on as much as adults do. Forget school dances or spelling bees. And forget letters from losers, like the advice column Megan had started running in *Real News*. Snore. Major REMs. But that's the sort of silliness Megan O'Connor, Princess of Pink, calls news.

Headlines floated through my mind:

PULITZER GOES TO COVERAGE OF MIDDLE-SCHOOL DANCE!

SEPTEMBER STOMP SENDS ECHOES ROUND THE WORLD!

I don't think so.

"You've got mail!" the computer announced cheerfully. Gotta love that voice.

I clicked on the mail icon, and Griffin's response filled the screen.

TO: Wordpainter
FROM: Thebeast
RE: What makes Casey tick?

I'm calling your bluff. This Pulitzer campaign is a total fraud! You say you want a prize, but we both know why you're such a talented reporter. You want kids to hear the truth.

Keep chasing that knock-your-socks-off story. (You can't help yourself, I know.)

But don't look over your shoulder for the prize patrol. What really matters to you is getting the word out.

I hate it when he pulls me up short like that. I opened my reporter's journal and began writing. . . .

Need (1) plan (2) story (3) crisis to cover (4) adventure (5) chocolate.

Hey, a girl can't be brilliant on thoughts alone.

My mind was clicking. But it was almost three thirty. Time for cheerleading tryouts.

You heard me. Not that *I* was planning to do any rah-rah jumps. In my book, cheerleaders, and the entire violent jock world they bounce around for, rate down there with the color pink, brussels sprouts and the gunk that sticks in the grooves on the bottom of sneakers.

But for some reason Ringo had decided to become Trumbull's first-ever male cheerleader.

MALE CROSSES CHEERLEADING GENDER GAP

A decent editorial, maybe. But award-winning material? Negative.

The things I'll do for a friend. Even for a weirdo like Ringo, who, best as I can tell, comes from the planet one planet beyond Jupiter. But that's what I like most about Ringo—his strangeness. Even if sitting around getting splinters in my butt while I watched airheads blast out inspirational chants wasn't my idea of fun.

I closed down the office, bought a chocolate bar from the machines outside the gym and plunged into the autumn sunshine. Despite my lack of an earth-shattering story, it was a nice day.

That is, until I walked through the gate and cut along the edge of the football field.

Hulking players clustered on the field. Their fat padding and shiny helmets made them look like large stuffed animals.

TEN-TON MONKEYS TAKE FIELD
They Grunt: Football!

Now *that* would be a sports story I'd actually agree to write.

I knew that somewhere out there was Gary Williams. Gary writes all the sports stories for *Real News*. He's also on the football team. No surprise there. His muscles are almost as big as his ego. However, Gary spends more time on the bench than on the field. The upside? A permanent place on the sidelines gives Gary time to zero in on the play-by-play for *Real News*. Not my idea of killer journalism, but someone had to do it.

I trudged over to the neighboring soccer field, where half a dozen cheerleaders swarmed around a long table that had been set up on the sidelines. In their red-and-white pleated skirts and sweaters, they looked like bizarro candy canes.

I tried to ignore the voice inside my head that screamed: ESCAPE! NOW! Three squares of chocolate later, I could breathe again.

From what I could tell, tryouts hadn't started yet. Girls with numbers pinned to their chests were scattered around the field chanting and practicing their routines: Stomping. Jumping. Waving pom-poms.

"Let's go, Tigers, go!
Let's fight, Tigers, fight!
Let's win, Tigers, win!
Go! Fight! Win!"

Cough! Gag! One girl's cheer came floating over the air like poison gas.

REPORTER COLLAPSES FROM OVERDOSE OF SCHOOL SPIRIT

Was I going to lose my friend to *this*?

My palms were sweating. My chocolate bar was melting. Just when I thought I would have to make a run for it, I spotted him. The kid in the baggy sweats, tie-dyed sweatshirt and bright-red bandanna.

Ringo. Warm gray eyes. Shiny brown hair just long enough to tuck behind his ears. A smile too goofy to be fake.

I saw a swirl of tie-dye as he spun a cartwheel. Then he kicked his legs out like an open scissors, and followed it with a very impressive boy-quality backflip. Did I mention that he has Jell-O for bones?

He was catching his breath when I caught up to him. "That scissor-leg thing was so happening."

"The herkie." Ringo retied his bandanna, tucking his chestnut hair underneath it. "It's an anti-gravity thing. Kind of lunar, with a chili-pepper twist."

A girl in spiffy white shorts and a red shirt with the number 6 pinned on it pranced over. "Fab herkie, Ringo!" she squealed, lifting her red sunglasses. Even her fingernails were red and white. "I think it's great that a guy is trying out for the squad. I really, *really* hope you make it."

And I really, *really* wished this girl would go away. Maybe to Iowa . . . or Mars. I snapped off another row of chocolate squares. For my nerves.

"Thanks, Samantha," Ringo said. "I appreciate—"

"Excuse us." Grabbing Ringo's sweatshirt just below the number 3, I pulled him a few feet away. "Are you sure you want to go through with this?" I whispered. "Seriously, Ringo. Trust me."

I was *trying* to be supportive, but hitting people straight on with my Big Opinions is something that happens before I can stop myself. The look on his face confirmed I had said too much, so I held out my peace offering. Chocolate. "Want some?"

Ringo popped a square into his mouth and chewed thoughtfully. "Friends," he said. "It's just like the human pyramid, you know? Sometimes the geometry is there. Everyone's in the right spot, holding up everyone else . . ." Ringo licked some melted chocolate from his fingers. "But at any moment one part could crumble and the whole thing falls into shapelessness."

He lost me, but just then the head cheerleader announced that tryouts were starting. It kept me from inserting my brown Converse any farther down my throat. "Good luck, Ringo," I said.

And surprise, surprise. I really meant it.

Just as I climbed up to the highest bleachers and sat down, a pumped-up football jersey materialized next to me. I looked past the chin guard and saw big almond eyes, cheeks the color of hot chocolate, and short black baby dreadlocks that were squishing out from inside the helmet. Gary Williams.

If you ask me, a guy who lives for sports is about as appealing as the mold we grow in petri dishes in science class. But for some reason, a lot of girls think Gary is cute. Whatever.

"Gary!" Ringo hollered, waving. The only boy in a line of about thirty girls, he definitely stood out.

"Geez! Use a megaphone, why don't you?" Gary said under his breath. He bent forward, burying his helmet in his hands. "If the guys think

I'm buds with a dude who wants to be a cheerleader, I'll be a total joke."

Did I mention that Gary is about as enlightened as a rock in a cave?

A handful of other stuffed football jerseys wandered our way to watch Number 1 as she shouted out a cheer. Extra school spirit. Hold the individuality.

Finally it was Ringo's turn. He jogged over to the judges' table wearing his patented goofy grin.

"Yo! Number three! Where's your skirt?" one beefy linebacker called out.

Down on the field, Ringo's smile faltered for a second. But only for a second. Then he started cheering: "Red! White! Tigers, let's fight . . ."

"Nice moves, pop tart," another kid shouted. "Do you shave your legs, too?"

Gary tugged his helmet as far forward over his face as it would go. "What a disaster . . ." He started down the bleachers.

"Great show of support, Gar," I called after him. Sure, I was seriously allergic to this scene, too. But Ringo needed us.

I cupped my hands around my mouth and shouted to the jock, "Hey, Hercules! I think you left your brain in the locker room."

I didn't know cheerleaders were allowed to

glare, but the head candy cane flashed me a decent one as she picked up a megaphone from the judges' table. "Quiet, please!"

The players kept their heckling down for the rest of Ringo's tryout. He shouted out two cheers, complete with jumps and styling dance moves. For his finale: the Ringo Flip. Not bad. By the time he was finished, so was my chocolate. Why hadn't I bought two?

Ringo's motor was still running as he bounded up into the stands and straddled the bench beside me. "So? What did you think?" he asked, cheeks flushed.

Somehow I managed to strangle the words that wanted to fly out of my mouth: *Forget all this and let's go find a killer story!*

Instead, I said, "I'm not exactly an expert, Ringo. But in the opinion of someone who would rather sort paper clips than support tackle sports? You looked good."

"I admit, I got a little thrown," Ringo said. He grabbed his backpack, pulled out his spiral notebook and a pen and started drawing.

Ringo is always doodling. Mostly he draws Simon, this way weird cartoon dude who is a lot like—you guessed it—way weird Ringo. A few strokes of the pen, and boom. Instant Simon.

Mirror, mirror, on the wall...who's...?

"What were those guys yelling about?" he asked.

"Something about manly men, I think. But it's hard to be sure. I don't speak Pig Grunt."

Chewing his pen, Ringo stared at the football field. "Who decided *they're* the real guys? Did somebody make a list I don't know about?"

"Don't let the Muscle Squad get to you," I said as I shifted my butt on the hard bleacher. "Exercise your freedom of will. Go for it!" I told him. But then I couldn't help myself. "It's not just the *cheerleading* thing I have a problem with, it's the whole jock enchilada. I'm all for a good game of basketball in the driveway or a killer bike ride. But when there's tackling and grunting involved—no thanks."

I swung my hand out toward the football field like a showroom model. "Just look what can happen when you spend too much time in the Jock Zone. Check out the tyrant coach."

I pointed to a man in a red-and-white team jacket on the field. He was all over a blond kid who held his helmet under one arm. Fingers in the face. Barking voice. Flailing arms. "A beautiful display of sportsmanship. Football is one useless endeavor. You can almost see the testosterone flying in the air."

"Where?" Ringo ducked, an alarmed look in his eyes.

"I think we're safe here."

Down on the sidelines, the coach kept snarling at the kid. "Aaw, don't be an idiot! You think I got time for this? Do you? *Do you?*"

The blond kid frowned down at the ground.

"What are you, afraid?" barked the coach. "Be a man, Chris. Get in there and show your stuff! Kill! Kill! Kill! That's the name of the game!"

"Talk about pressure," I said. "It's a *practice* for a *sport*. I thought sports were about having fun, not winning at any cost." I nodded at the field. "'Be a man'? What's that supposed to mean?"

"Exactly," said Ringo. "Why couldn't he be a man if he planted a flower? Or found a lost kitten?"

I couldn't take my eyes off the kid on the field. Chris was maybe twelve, thirteen max.

And probably mortified that all his teammates were watching him get chewed out, big time. Chris pulled on his helmet as if he were strapping on a ten-ton weight. Not that the coach noticed or cared. He slapped Chris on the back and pushed him back onto the field. "You think this is tough? I'll show you pain! Be a man!"

"Barbaric," I muttered. "What an ego trip."

"My family took an eco-trip last summer," Ringo said. "Cross-country. We hit all the major butterfly farms and bird sanctuaries . . ."

I tuned out.

I was too busy listening to the alarm that had gone off inside my head. The alarm that signaled I was onto a story.

Fish Out of Water
Heaves Last Gasp

I WAS ALL for hanging out with Ringo at the Hole-in-the-Mall after tryouts. Moral support and all that. But I hadn't counted on a bunch of perfectly ponytailed girls coming with us. At the moment, they dangled around our table like ornaments.

"Congrats, everyone! We made it through the hard part," said the girl with black bangs in her eyes. The one who'd drooled over Ringo before tryouts. What was her name? Sahara? Samantha? Salmonella? Something like that. Her red-and-white fingernails clinked against the glass as she lifted it in the air.

There were giggles all around as the girls raised their soda glasses. Even Ringo was grinning.

I was there for Ringo. That was what I kept telling myself. But I was gasping for air. A fish out of water.

The girl next to me shifted so the back of her warm-up jacket was in my face. Did I have ketchup on my chin? Or was she afraid I might contaminate her brain with an actual thought?

"Ringo," I suddenly blurted out. "I've got a story idea. Kids who want to rebel against the militant orders coaches give them." I leaned across the table and grabbed one of his fries. "The headline? KIDS TELL COACH TO DROP AND GIVE 'EM TWENTY!"

"Cool, Casey." Ringo sipped his shake and turned to a blond girl beside him. "I think the judges liked your voice quality, Monica. Do you do vocal warm-ups?"

I had lost him.

"Too bad most of the spots were filled last year. There are only two spots for sixth graders," said a girl with braces. She smacked Ringo's arm lightly, as if they were best buds. "I don't know *what* I'll do if I don't make it."

Uh, get a life?

"Casey! Ringo! Hi!" a cheery voice piped up.

Megan O'Connor.

As if I wasn't already over my head in cuteness and color coordination. Here was my own

17

personal Sugarplum Fairy. With her perk wand.

I turned and blinked. Today she almost looked like a fairy. It wasn't just the rhinestone butterfly clip in her perfectly trimmed blond hair. She was also wearing a blue jacket with sheer, luminescent sleeves. It was actually a little flashy for preppy Megan.

"Was there a sale at Glitter World?" I asked.

"No, I wasn't shopping," Megan said. She wasn't even close to getting it. "I've been rehearsing for next Friday's show. You know, *Collages*? It's this series of student performances. Each piece is different, but when you put them together they make a glorious whole. A collage!"

In addition to being editor of *Real News*, Megan belongs to a handful of different clubs. Including Drama Club. Almost every rah-rah girl at my table said hi to her. That figured. Everyone knew perky, popular Megan.

"I love collages." Ringo put down his shake and reached for some fries. "The way you can make a picture out of old scraps—sort of like recycled art. And then, you can cut up the collage and start over again. Infinity art."

"I didn't know you were in the show," I said.

Megan's cheeks grew pink. Make that pinker. "I'm not actually *in* the show," she confessed. "I mean, sixth graders almost never get parts. Not big parts, anyway. But I'm helping Anna Zafrani learn her lines."

She nodded toward a table. One look and I understood Megan's twinkle-toes costume. One girl wore this bizarro red hat that was a cross between Red Riding Hood and Sherlock Holmes. Another girl wore an oversized man's jacket with cuffs folded a million times and a carnation in the buttonhole.

Major costuming. Except this was how the drama crowd dressed all the time. Think they liked to be noticed? Nobody wears a red hat like that, even to cover up a bad-hair day.

I secretly dug their adventurous sense of style.

Somewhere behind the scripts and baskets of fries and onion rings I recognized Anna Zafrani. Her black hair was braided into a swirl on top of her head. And a pair of sunglasses hung on the neck of her red sweater—the Zafrani trademark. I imagined her sleeping with sunglasses clipped to her flannel nightgown.

Usually I try not to pay attention to the popularity pyramid. But Megan had made a huge fuss over Anna Zafrani in Drama Club photos. Anna *was* the Drama Club. The president. The queen. The star.

"I'd better get back," Megan said.

"Right," I muttered. "Anna might need more ketchup with her fries."

Megan's brows lifted. "What's that supposed to mean?"

That you're slaving away for an eighth grader just to be popular? It's not always easy to sneak a snarky comment past Megan. So I answered: "Go. Rehearse. Ooze. We'll try to look the other way."

For a second Megan stared at me. Then a bright smile lit her face. "You are too much, Casey."

I hate it when she does that.

I meditated on the last of Ringo's fries and dived into my journal and wrote:

kids and sports—how many kids really want to play? How far should a coach push?

I looked up as a jock wave washed into Hole-in-the-Mall. A sea of football jackets, muscle and major attitude. Of course, Gary floated in the center of it.

To my journalistic delight, I spotted the player the coach had yelled at over by the video games.

"There he is." I nudged Ringo. "The kid who

was getting muscled by that coach. What was his name? Chris?"

Something was wrong with the kid's jacket. It wasn't zipped up. He slid it off with one arm, and I saw that the other arm was bandaged.

"Ringo!" I grabbed his elbow. "Is that a *sling* on his arm?"

Ringo nodded. "Maybe some of that flying testosterone you were talking about hit him."

Something buzzed inside my head. Call it a reporter's instinct, but I get a clear signal when a there's a story hanging in the air.

Grabbing my journal, I made a beeline for Gary, who was waiting in line to order food.

"Who's the kid in the sling?" I asked. "That Chris guy. I saw him at practice."

Gary shrugged off his football jacket. "*You* watched practice? So you're turning into a fan?"

"In your dreams. I just heard the kid getting grilled, that's all. What's his name?" I asked again, my pen poised over my journal.

"You mean Chris Slater," Gary said. "He's second-string, like me. His dad is the assistant coach."

His dad?

There was definitely something here. "It looked like his father was pushing him pretty hard," I said.

Gary shrugged. "Coach Slater can be pretty tough. No pain, no gain."

I hate those pat words of advice, like "You live, you learn." But I decided to save that tirade for another time. "Chris definitely looks like he's in pain," I pointed out, moving up to the counter with Gary. "So what was the deal during practice? Chris didn't seem too thrilled about playing."

"He wasn't. But the thing is—"

"Who's next?" the girl behind the counter called.

"Two cheeseburgers and a shake," Gary answered.

I wouldn't have minded a burger, but it was pizza night at home and I was saving myself for a real Italian pig-out. But my growling stomach didn't stop me from getting in Gary's face when he was done ordering.

"So, what went on out there?" I probed. "Do coaches always force kids to play like that?"

"They don't force anyone," Gary said defensively. "This is different, Casey. The coach is—"

"His father," I interrupted. "And that gives him the right to trample over Chris's freedom of choice?"

"I didn't say that." Gary gave a frustrated tug to his baseball cap. "What's going on, Casey?"

"I'm not sure yet." Ignoring Gary's wary look,

I added, "Come on. Introduce me to Chris."

Gary grabbed a straw and some packets of ketchup, frowning. "No way. We're just here to hang out, Casey. What gives?"

"What do you think?" I checked out the video scene. Chris was hanging by the games, watching other guys play. "Come on, Gar. Help me out here."

Gary dropped the packets of ketchup onto his tray. "Not a chance. We just spent an hour and a half getting flak from the coaches. You think Chris'll want to be cross-examined by some girl who can't tell the difference between a football and a basketball?"

Probably not. But that had never stopped me before. I took a deep breath—a major whiff of fast-food euphoria. Gets me every time. Did I have the nerve to jump into the jock fray and introduce myself?

I marched right up to Chris and said, "Hi, I'm Casey Smith. Gary works with me on the paper, and I couldn't help but notice your injury. So what happened? Hurt your arm during a tip-off?"

"You mean a *kickoff*," Gary corrected. He had followed me with his tray of food. "Tip-offs are in basketball, Casey."

"Whatever."

Chris winced as someone bumped into him.

"I pulled a shoulder muscle at home yesterday. I probably shouldn't have played today, but . . ." He stopped in midsentence. "Anyway, no big deal."

He eased away from me, then headed over to join some other players at a table.

"Now can I eat?" Gary glared at me. "Your sniffer is way off here, Casey. The deep fryers must be clogging your nostrils."

I didn't answer as he headed back to the counter. I didn't want to tell him that he was wrong. *Way* wrong.

I knew this for sure: Chris hadn't given me all the facts. But I could fill in the blanks.

He had come to the practice with an injury.

His dad had pushed him to play.

And now his arm was even worse, all because his dad wanted him to "be a man" on the football field.

PARENTS WHO PRESSURE KIDS FOR PEAK PERFORMANCE IN SPORTS: Is the Price Too High?

I was going to blow the jocks off the field with this one.

Story Shot Down by SCUD Missile

WHEN I WALKED into the *Real News* room for the staff meeting on Monday morning, I was ready. I had my scoop, my notes, my angle. I'd even worn a baseball cap to pitch my big sports story.

Okay, my big *anti*-sports story.

I guess it was the day for headgear. Toni Velez, our staff photographer, had this chain of plastic spiders wrapped around her ponytail. They jiggled around her springy orange hair as she pored over the photos spread across the table in front of her.

I dropped my backpack onto Dalmatian Station, the name Ringo came up with for our lime-green table with black polka dots. "Where is everyone?" I asked.

"How should I know?" Toni said crisply. Her

hair cascaded around her face as she looked up from her contact sheet. "Do I look like a Scout leader?"

Smell the attitude? And this was a *good* mood. Trust me. Toni is not someone you want to cross. Picture a hungry tiger. Actually, today she was wearing this shiny orange-and-black sweatshirt with a sort of tiger-stripe thing going on. That, over military-type pants and lace-up boots. And a look that said: You got a problem? Well, it ain't mine.

I admired Toni. But more than that, when it came to photos, Toni had the right stuff. That counted. She was afraid of nothing and no one. Of course, her fearless qualities sometimes made it difficult to have her on staff. Not that I was angling for a bunch of warm, cuddly Megan clones.

We both felt the whirlwind that blasted into the room. Enter Ringo with his lucky red bandanna wrapped around his head like a brain bandage. He jumped on top of the spotted table and sat cross-legged like a happy Buddha.

"Go ahead! Smell me!" He said it like he was offering a free trip to Disney World.

Toni's eyebrows shot up as she saved a photo from Ringo's Birkenstocks. "Say what?"

"His brain cells are dying," I said. "A known side effect of cheerleading."

"I read somewhere that animals can smell the fear in a person," Ringo said. "And the triumph."

Right at that moment, I got it. "You made the cheerleading squad?"

Ringo nodded, beaming.

"Go, guy!" Toni whooped. A dozen bracelets jingled on her arm as she gave Ringo a high five.

REPORTER LOSES FRIEND TO GIGGLE SQUAD

Okay, I was happy for him. Sort of. "Promise me you won't belt out cheers during staff meetings," I begged. "I mean, just because you're on the squad now—"

"Actually, I made alternate," Ringo said. "I only cheer if someone else can't make it."

"Congratulations, Ringo." Megan's chipper voice came from the doorway.

She and Gary hustled into the room, carrying a heavy stack of newspapers between them. "The first male cheerleader ever at Trumbull. That's great!"

"Pathetic," Gary groaned. Ringo slid off the table as Gary dropped the newspapers onto Dalmatian Station with a *thunk*.

Megan went into neatnik overdrive, brushing imaginary dirt from her hands and red jumper.

27

Then she took the power spot—the chair that didn't wobble.

Mr. Baxter, our faculty advisor, danced into the room. For a guy who looks like he's gone way overboard on the donuts, he's pretty light on his feet. He tapped the pile of newspapers with a thick finger.

"Looks like I got here just in time to sample our latest issue of *Real News*," he said.

Megan nodded. "Fresh from the printer. Gary and I just picked it up from the office." Grabbing a pair of scissors that lay next to Toni's photos, she found the exact center of the cord that bound the bundle, then snipped through it. "One of our best issues ever!" she chirped, handing out copies to the rest of us.

Of course, Megan always says that.

She glowed as she turned the pages. Watching the way she smoothed the wrinkles out of each one made me wince. Even the way she read the paper was prissy. I knew exactly what she was looking for, too. JAM. That's short for Just Ask Megan. The gooey advice column Megan had insisted on running.

"Super!" Megan enthused. "You guys worked really hard on this issue. It's so easy to criticize, but sometimes we don't take enough time to remind each other that our hard work is paying off."

"Spare me," I groaned. "Shouldn't we be talking about *next* week's paper?"

"Come on, Casey," Megan said, turning another page and meticulously smoothing it. "Don't you ever take the time to enjoy what we've accomplished?"

"Occasionally." The truth? I've probably read over our old issues 25 bazillion times. But I'd sooner shave my head than admit that to Megan.

"Are we having a meeting or an ego-fest?" I asked.

"Right." Megan closed the newspaper, realizing that reading her own column in front of the staff was pretty tacky. "Okay, let's get started. Casey?"

I was good to go. "Pressure on kids to perform in sports," I said, doffing my baseball cap for effect. I found the page in my journal where I'd written:

Participation ↑

Injuries ↑

"I've been on the Net. I've checked the stats for middle-school teams. Participation is up, but so are injuries. They've risen steadily over the last few years. Kids need to know the dangers of giving in to that kind of pressure. The damage to their bodies could plague them for the rest of their lives."

"Where's the hook for Trumbull?" Megan asked.

The "hook" is the special angle that makes the story right for our school.

"We've got walking wounded right here," I said. "Coach Slater pressured his son Chris to play football with an injured shoulder, and now it's worse. I'm sure Chris isn't the only one. I want to do interviews—"

"Why the anti-sports angle?" Gary cut in, bending to tug at the laces of his hightops. "Just because you think one parent went too far doesn't mean you have to give *all* sports a bad name."

"It *is* kind of . . . negative," Megan said uncertainly.

"You think anything that doesn't come equipped with a smiley face is negative, Megan," I shot back. I pulled the list of Pulitzer stories from the front of my journal and handed it to her. "Earthquakes and bank robberies aren't exactly heartwarming, either. But those stories won awards. *Real* stories. This is relevant. And it's happening *right here at Trumbull*."

Ringo looked up from the doodle he was making in his notebook. "There was a bank robbery at Trumbull?" he asked.

"Not all of these are negative," Megan said, running a perfectly manicured finger down the list of Pulitzer winners. "What about the *New York Times* journalist who won for 'elegantly written stories about contemporary America'? Or this reporter for *The Wall Street Journal* who wrote about the accomplishments of inner-city honor students? Why can't you write about something like that?"

"Sure, and I can change my name to Chloe and take up snowboarding, too."

"You never know," Ringo cut in. "I read about this snowboarder who says the sport saved his life. Something about all that whiteness . . ."

"I just don't think *Real News* should be a downer for kids," Megan said, ignoring Ringo.

"Or maybe it was a surfboarder and the color was blue . . ." Ringo went on, ignoring Megan.

"Look, Megan," I said, trying to get the conversation back on track. "We're not all here to write horoscopes and dance reviews and weepy columns like JAM."

"I love jam," Toni cracked, her amber eyes shining. "Raspberry on toast."

"My favorite jams are flannel. Fire-engine red,"

Ringo said, still drawing in his notebook.

"JAM, that's the answer," I went on. "I'm sure a clever answer to some big-time whiner will win me a Pulitzer. . . ."

Oops. There were those flying words again. It can be a problem sometimes. Okay. Make that a lot of the time. Like now.

I didn't realize how far I'd gone until I saw the angry look in Megan's eyes. I shut my mouth.

"Focus, guys," said Mr. Baxter, with a pointed look at me. "Casey, isn't what you're pitching similar to Gary's story on Cal Pillson? The one we just ran?"

Ouch. That hurt.

GIRL REPORTER'S STORY SHOT DOWN, EGO PLUMMETS

"Gary's story was about pressure from coaches, not parents," I pointed out, trying to salvage my reputation and trying not to notice Gary's sudden intent listening. "Injuries weren't even an issue." I sounded firm, but all of a sudden I wasn't feeling quite so sure of myself.

"Pressure on kids in sports. It's too close," Mr. Baxter said. "You can do better."

He had a point. But somehow, I couldn't let go of the image tattooed inside my brain: Chris

Slater getting slammed by his dad.

"You wanna borrow my snowboard?" Ringo asked me. "We could meditate on the great white and open our minds to self-improvement."

"I don't think anything can improve your rep now, Ringo," Gary muttered, pushing up the sleeves of his polo shirt. "Ow!" he yelped as I shot him a swift kick under the table. "What was that for?"

"I think what Gary's trying to say," Mr. Baxter cut in, "is that we're all proud of you for making the cheerleading squad, Ringo." His belly mushed over the tabletop as he leaned forward. "I'm sure Mr. Williams would like to show his support by covering the story for our next issue."

"What!" Gary's dreads snapped in the air as he spun to gape at Mr. Baxter.

"That's a great idea!" Megan made a note in her neat, looping script. "What else do you have, Gary?"

He passed two typewritten pages across the table to her. "For our clubs feature. Profile of the swim team. Ahead of schedule," he gloated.

Whoop-dee-doo. *Another* sports story.

"Super!" Megan made a check on her clipboard. Another piece of her life, squeezed into one of her orderly little boxes.

"And tomorrow night—football." Gary did a

drumroll on the polka-dotted table. "Deergrass and Trumbull, league rivals, meet after dark. I'll do a background piece on the competition between the schools, profiles of the top players from both teams, and a play-by-play from the game."

"What about photos?" Toni asked.

"Full-page spread," Gary answered. "The game's at Deergrass. My dad can give us a ride."

"Your dad? Ugh, thanks, but I'm already covered." Toni's rings clanked as she waved Gary off. "My friend Jenna's boyfriend has a car."

Boyfriend? Car? My brain could barely absorb the words. Toni seemed a step ahead of the herd, sure. But she was still in the sixth grade, like the rest of us. Stuck around eleven-year-old boys, who are not exactly crush material. I mean, when a guy is fixated on computers and jokes about toe jam or oozing brains, what's to like?

True, there are a few exceptions. My long-distance best friend Griffin is a totally normal person. And then there's Tyler McKenzie. But we are not, I repeat, *not* talking about Tyler McKenzie.

"You know someone who goes with a high school guy?" Megan asked Toni.

"No biggie." Toni shrugged. "Jenna Randazzo. She's in the eighth grade. She sees this guy AJ

34

who's, like, sixteen. Drives this Camaro."

Mr. Baxter leaned forward, his brows furrowed. You know the expression: Concerned Adult Look. "Do your parents know who you're going with?" he asked.

"They're cool with it," Toni said, rolling her eyes as if to say: *Back off, Baxter.*

"Well . . ."

The bell rang, and Toni was spared Mr. Baxter's lecture. Everyone started packing up and moving out.

Everyone except Ringo. A shock of hair escaped from his bandanna as he bent over page 6 of the paper. "Maybe *I* should write to JAM," he said. "About how being a guy cheerleader is no big deal."

"Hello?" I knocked on the table. "JAM is Just Ask Megan. You can talk to her anytime, Ringo."

Toni slipped the last of her photos into a manila envelope. "Girl's got a point," she said. Jewelry jingled as she hitched her backpack onto her shoulder and darted out the door behind Gary and Mr. Baxter.

"But why would you want *Megan's* advice?" I continued. "Now that you're a cheerleader, do you need help sorting your socks by color and size?"

Letting out a long sigh, Ringo took his pen and whipped off a few fluid lines. He showed me the result:

I've lost something.... Maybe it's me.

I got the picture—no pun intended. I realized I was dissing Ringo at every turn. "I'm going to be a pillar of support from now on. I promise. You don't need to become one of the losers who write in to JAM."

I was aware of Megan listening from across the room. But did that stop me?

Get real.

I decided to skim the JAM column. IGNORED wants to know how to get the boy in math class to notice her again. Loser league. PUNISHED doesn't know how to convince her parents her curfew is unreasonable. My advice in three words? *Talk to them*.

"Read one out loud," Ringo said.

"Okay, here's one from I KNOW HE CARES. Probably some quivering mouse who eats heart-shaped cereal for breakfast." Holding back a snicker, I read on:

> "Sometimes someone I really love
> gets mad when I mess things up.
> He doesn't understand that I can't
> help it. When I screw up, he goes
> wild. He hits me. Sometimes it's
> really bad. It's hard to hide the
> bruises."

"Whoa . . ." I said, kind of to myself. This was intense. And there was more:

> "I don't want to make him
> madder. I just want him to stop
> hitting me. I know he cares about
> me. He doesn't mean to hurt me,
> and I don't want to get him in
> trouble. How can I get him to
> stop hitting me?"

Ringo just stared at his drawing. Silently, I

reread the letter. This wasn't the sniveling complaint of a loser. This kid was hurting.

Big time.

"Well, Casey?" Megan asked, breaking the silence. "Still think advice columns are for whiny losers?"

I heard the prim, I-told-you-so tone in her voice. Background noise to the image that had started rerunning inside my head: Chris Slater, suffering through a verbal beating by his dad. And later, with his arm in a sling, wincing in pain.

Maybe that shoulder injury hadn't been an accident, as Chris had claimed. Maybe words weren't the only things Mr. Slater hit his kid with. Maybe Chris had written this letter because his dad beat him.

CHAPTER 4

Desperately Seeking Person

ONE THING ABOUT us bulldog reporter types: Once we sink our teeth into something, we can't let go.

Maybe I get it from my grandmother. She's a journalist, like me. (Well, add thirty years of reporting experience, a Pulitzer, several Emmys, and a few books. You get the idea.) Usually, Gram lives in New York City, but she had been staying with me for the last few months, while my parents and big brother were in Southeast Asia. It's cool having her around. She knows her stuff.

My parents are part of a program called Doctors Without Borders. Right now they're working with victims of a huge explosion in this chemical plant. My sixteen-year-old brother Billy? Let's just say he's along for the ride—and a little extra tutoring.

Hey, I never said my family was conventional. Families today come in all flavors. Sherlocking with the who, what, when, where, and why of Big Issues is our family tradition.

Speaking of Holmes, I already had the "what" for my new story—physical abuse. Of someone right here in Trumbull. Definitely a story that got under the skin. But why? Where? When?

I wasn't even close. Much less to the big question: Who?

Chris Slater? I had to find out. I made a detour to the main lobby before math class. The box for JAM letters was there on a table. I figured if Chris had written once, he might write again.

I groaned when I saw the poster tacked up behind the box. It had all the Megan ingredients: glitter, smiley faces, exclamation points. JUST ASK MEGAN!!!!

I was so glad I hadn't eaten lunch yet.

Then I saw the padlock. Apparently, all that glitter hadn't blinded Megan's practical side. She'd made the box tamper-resistant.

I picked it up and shook it. Empty.

Was that because no one had written to JAM since last week? Or had Megan just retrieved the letters?

Too bad I couldn't get the answer right away. I had to suffer through complex fractions and field hockey before I could track down Megan and Chris during lunch. By the time I made it to the cafeteria, I felt intensely impatient. But I'm good at that.

I scanned the backs of heads in the lunch line. No sign of a blond-haired boy wearing a sling. And I didn't spot Megan's blond hair or red velvet scrunchie—the one that matched her red jumper, naturally.

"'Scuse me," a boy mumbled as he angled past me.

I glanced up just as he looked at me.

Tyler McKenzie.

We both froze.

You want my big confession? Okay, here it is. Tyler is someone I kind of like. I'm talking brown hair, eyes the color of semisweet chocolate, and a smile that mushed my knees.

Except that smile hadn't been aimed at me for a while.

To make a long story short, I wrote a story that ruined Tyler's life. At least, that's how he saw it. But how was I supposed to know Tyler's dad would lose his job because of my superior investigative skills?

For half a second I thought I saw . . . Was that a smile? Not a full-blown, weak-in-the-knees flash. But maybe the tiniest I-don't-*totally*-hate-you smirk.

Then Tyler just sort of blinked and walked away.

PIANO DROPS FROM SKY
Girl Reporter Flattened

I had heard that Mr. McKenzie was working again, teaching at a community college. But I guess Tyler still held a grudge. Then again, that could have been interpreted as an almost-smile. Right?

"You looking for an empty table?" Ringo asked, breaking my daze as he danced by balancing a carton of milk and a sandwich on top of his spiral notebook.

"Nope. I'm looking for Megan." I shoved my lunch bag on top of my math book, trying not to notice where Tyler sat. Which was at a table in the back where two of his buddies were arm wrestling over a bag of chips. I definitely was *not* paying attention.

"Or Chris Slater," I said distractedly. "I need to talk to him, too."

Ringo squinted. "No sign of Megan. Or Chris. Maybe they're having an out-of-body experience. But there's Samantha with some of the girls on the squad. Want to sit with them?"

GIRL REPORTER LOST IN BARF ZONE

"Right. And maybe I should just replace my brains with the inside of my peanut butter and jelly sandwich. Come on." I tugged his denim sleeve toward the door. "We've got better things to do. Like finding Megan and getting the real deal on Chris."

"My aunt Rita is always getting deals," Ringo said as we bailed the cafeteria. "Last year she traded a crate of oranges for a Volvo."

I didn't even try to get onto his Web site. I was on a mission. "Maybe Megan's in the *Real News* room. Or Gary. He might know what's going on with Chris." I led the way down the hall.

"She rebuilt the engine and it was good as new," Ringo went on. "But now it makes me wonder. Did anyone ever say to Aunt Rita, 'Sorry, fixing cars is a guy thing'? Did people tell her she should be a cheerleader instead of a car mechanic just because she's a woman?" Ringo was on a roll.

I glanced at Ringo as we came to the newsroom. "Are we talking about cheerleading or Volvos?"

He shrugged. "Forget it."

Just then I spotted Gary inside the newsroom. I marched over and sat at the desk next to him. "I need to know something about Chris Slater."

Gary's eyes flashed with annoyance. He didn't

bother looking up from his salami sandwich and chips.

"Back off, Casey."

Not a piece of advice I have ever taken seriously. "It's about Chris's shoulder," I said. "And his dad. Maybe you can help me talk to Chris about—"

"What for?" Gary cut in. "So you can write that story even though Mr. Baxter told you not to? So he can see what a brilliant reporter you are and beg your forgiveness for ever having trashed your idea?"

I gaped at him. Gary wasn't just sulking. He was mad. At *me*. "Did I wear the wrong deodorant today or something?" I asked. "What's the matter?"

"What's the matter," he said quietly. "What's the matter?" Now his voice was incredulous.

"Hey, I asked first. Now you're supposed to answer. Something like, 'Casey, I hate it when you lace your sneakers backwards.'"

"Like it's a joke? Just forget it." His chair scraped back as he shot to his feet.

"Gary—"

"No." Grabbing his chips, he blew past Ringo and me and was out the door.

I called after him. "Was it something I said?"

School Police Raid Student Files

"GARY?" I CALLED again.

No answer. He was history. All that was left of him was the plastic wrap from his sandwich.

"Hey, guys," Megan said, popping into the room. She picked up a sandwich from her lunch. "Any new leads on a front-page story?"

"I've got a new angle to run by you," I told her, reaching into my crumpled bag for a PBJ.

"All about Chris Slater and real deals," Ringo piped up, tearing open his sandwich wrapper. "Or was it out-of-body experiences?"

Megan took a dainty sip from her juice box before setting it down next to the perfectly square, uneaten corner of her cheese sandwich. "Sounds scattered."

"First, I've got some questions for you," I said,

pointing to Megan. "Burning questions. Scorchers."

She wriggled her eyebrows. "I'm dying to hear them. But I've got to run. I promised to paint scenery for *Collages*." Megan finished chewing her sandwich, then folded her lunch bag and tucked it in the recycle bin. "Why don't you guys come? We could use the help."

"Scenery?" I echoed, considering the sizzling story I was on. "I'd rather spray graffiti in the boys' room."

"The boys' room could use some color," Ringo said. "But those tiles are so slippery. I'm in."

REPORTER'S FRIEND DEFECTS TO DRAMA CLUB

Great. "Go ahead, Ringo. Numb your brain with flowers and glitter."

"Why do you have to be so negative?" Megan shot back. "At least he's willing to try different things. That's a lot more than I can say for you." She grabbed her backpack from the floor, slid the strap over her shoulder and headed for the door. "Come on, Ringo."

"Not so fast," I said. Pushing my sandwich aside, I pulled a copy of *Real News* from my backpack. "I think you forgot something. Take another look at your answer to I KNOW HE CARES."

Snatching away the paper, she read the

response aloud. Not that she needed to. I had
memorized it:

> "If someone is hitting you,
> that's abuse. It's not your fault,
> and it's not okay. Ever. Making
> excuses for the violent person
> just makes it possible for him to
> go on hurting you.
>
> "But there are people who can
> help. . . ."

"Yeah, yeah," I interrupted. "And you suggest talking to friends, the school guidance counselor . . ."

"And I included the telephone number of a
support group," Megan finished.

"Right. But it's not enough," I said. "What if
the kid doesn't do any of the stuff you suggest?"

Megan's blue eyes were thoughtful as she
stared at the JAM column. "I hope the kid will
get help. After all, whoever it is reached out
to *me*."

"It's not enough." I shook my head. "We have
to reach out to that kid. And I think I know who
it is."

"That letter was anonymous," Megan said,
placing the newspaper on the desk. I could see

her frustration growing. "Whoever wrote it didn't sign it."

"I don't need neon letters spelling out the kid's name," I said. "I can read the clues: Chris Slater's dad has been using him as a verbal punching bag at practice. The kid's shoulder is injured. And . . ."

"Chris Slater?" Megan was thoughtful as she drummed her shiny fingernails against the desk.

"No wonder he wanted to get out of his body," Ringo said. Then he bit into his sandwich.

Megan shook her head slowly. "I don't think so. Besides, you shouldn't be trying to find out who it is. JAM is confidential."

"We have to *find* I KNOW HE CARES," I insisted. "It's up to us to *make sure* that kid gets help, whether it's Chris or someone else."

"No way," Megan said, tightening her grip on the strap. "The whole point of JAM is that people can be anonymous. Kids aren't going to write in if they think there's a chance of someone exposing them."

"Someone is being *hurt*, Megan. I'm going to find out who."

I crossed my arms over my chest, doing the body language thing. No way was I backing down.

I could just imagine myself scrutinizing the original letter under a magnifying glass. Maybe there'd be fingerprints. Or really distinctive hand-writing, like a backward slant or something. I could get a copy of Chris's handwriting and compare the two samples.

Squaring off with Megan, I delivered my demand. "I need to see the letter from I KNOW HE CARES," I said firmly. "The original."

"I'd like to see it, too," a voice spoke up from the hall.

You never saw three heads snap around so quickly. We all turned to see one of the school guidance counselors standing in the doorway, a shadowy woman in flowing pants and a long sweater, with a professionally concerned look on her face.

My palms began to sweat.

I had nothing against this counselor, whom I knew only vaguely. But the whole guidance thing bothered me. Why take your problems to a total stranger? And someone with the power to suspend you, too?

"Um, hi, Ms. Vermont," Megan said cautiously. "Is there something we can help you with?"

Leave it to Megan to actually *know* the woman.

"It's about your column, Megan." She gestured to Ringo and me. "Do you work on the paper, too?"

Now *that* hurt.

Megan introduced us.

"I'm here because I'm concerned," Ms. Vermont said. "I saw the letter from I KNOW HE CARES. Do you know who wrote it?"

Megan took a deep breath. "It's a confidential column."

"If a Trumbull student is being abused, I need to take action." Something flashed in her dark eyes. Something strong as steel. "That's my job."

Megan and I gaped as she stepped in and surveyed our newsroom.

Was she going to search the files?

Shut down the paper?

Frisk us?

"I came for that letter, Megan." She held out her hand. "May I have the original, please?"

Authorities Spill Jam!

THE LETTER?

"No way," I blurted out, curling my copy of *Real News* into a roll. I wasn't going to cave. And no way would I let Megan fold.

Sure, I wanted to see that letter, too. Big time. But this was different. This was about our rights as students and reporters.

"Every reporter has the right to keep a source confidential," I said, whacking my open palm with the rolled-up newspaper. "You can't have that letter."

As I spoke Megan turned and leaned over her desk.

Was she going for her files? Way to buckle under the pressure, JAM girl! Just hand over the file and wave bye-bye to Freedom of the Press.

"Casey and I were just going over this," Megan said. She grabbed the copy of *Real News* on the desk and handed it to Ms. Vermont. "I want you to know I didn't just whip off an answer. I did research. Is there a problem with something I wrote?"

Was it possible Megan wasn't a jelly-belly journalist, after all?

"Your advice is good, Megan," Ms. Vermont said. "But that's not the point. Do you have any idea what this child is dealing with? I've worked with abused kids and the truth is sometimes horrific. Sometimes . . ." She shook her head and her voice trailed off.

There was a heaviness in the air as she paused. Suddenly I realized that Ms. Vermont wasn't here to punish *us*. She just couldn't sit back while a student at Trumbull was being abused.

"Intervention may be the only way to protect the child," Ms. Vermont went on.

That threw Megan. Self-consciously, she reached up to make sure her scrunchie was still holding every hair in place. Was she stalling for time, or thinking of caving? "The person who wrote the letter didn't sign it," she finally said. "But . . . that's all I can tell you. I'm not going to give you the original."

What do you know? I wanted to throw my fist in the air and shout: *Yes! You go, Megan.* But I didn't think that would earn me any bonus points with Megan *or* Ms. Vermont.

"I don't think you understand how serious this is," said Ms. Vermont. "Some kids lie to get attention. It could be a prank. Or it could be a child with a serious disorder who's acting out. There are dozens of possibilities."

I took a moment to soak that up. The letter seemed so real.

"But what if the kid wrote to me because no one else believed him—or her?" Megan countered. "Kids are always overruled in the adult world. What if it's the victim's word against a grown-up's?"

Megan was rocking my world.

"There are ways to find out if a claim of abuse is true," Ms. Vermont persisted. "Talking to neighbors, tracing nine-one-one calls to the child's house. Even looking at hospital records to see if the child was treated in the ER. We can build a case. Or . . ." She gave Megan a sober glance.

"Or what?" Ringo spoke up for the first time. He'd been watching.

Ms. Vermont studied our faces carefully. "I'm afraid you're in over your heads, that's all."

"But the kid reached out to *me*," Megan pointed

out. "Anonymously. I can't compromise some-one's trust. Or privacy."

"Think about it." Ms. Vermont dropped the paper onto the desk. "Think of what might happen if this student needs more help than you can give."

She had a point. Megan and I exchanged a worried look. Were we in over our heads?

"I have to talk to Ms. Nachman about this," the counselor said. "She needs to know." Translation: You'll be summoned to the Principal's Office of Torture for further interrogation.

Ms. Vermont turned and floated down the hall in a swirl of loose pants and a long scarf.

Megan sighed and used her fingers to comb one side of her already perfect hair. "I wasn't sure she was going to let me off the hook," she said. "Thanks for backing me up, Casey."

BY-THE-BOOK EDITOR
GRATEFUL TO RENEGADE REPORTER
FOR BUCKING AUTHORITY

Definitely a first. Megan was probably just in shock from saying no to a grown-up.

"Freedom of the Press in action. Cool." Ringo tossed his sandwich wrapper in the trash and grabbed his notebook. "When's the scenery thing happening?"

"Five minutes ago!" The way Megan jumped for the doorway, you'd think she was late for a flight to Disney World.

"But we're not done yet, Megan!" I ran after her and Ringo, scribbling in my journal. Headlines. Story angles. They were bubbling up all around me:

SUPREME COURT RULES
FREEDOM OF PRESS APPLIES TO MIDDLE SCHOOL!
Girl Reporter Revolutionizes School Papers Nationwide!

Forget the sports story. I was onto something much bigger. And not just the faculty squashing our rights. A kid was being hit, bruised. Hurt.

GUIDANCE COUNSELOR STAGES ILLEGAL
RAID ON NEWSROOM
Free Press Threatened

I could just see Ms. Vermont and an army of teachers storming into the *Real News* office and raiding our files. Finding zilch, we reporters would then be questioned, one at a time, in a dark room, with just a chair and a lightbulb hanging over it.

"Casey Smith, reveal your sources or face seven years of detention for contempt of principal."

But I wouldn't cave. Not me. They could threaten me until the seventh grade, but . . .

I was still writing furiously in my journal when Megan and Ringo opened a door marked DRAMA. I caught it with my shoulder after they went through, pushing into a huge open room. There was a wall of windows, a glass booth and a stage. The place was a tangle of kids, cardboard scenery, paint cans and stacks of wood. There were also wardrobe racks stuffed with fabric and ugly frilly dresses, and boxes overflowing with hats, feather boas and mismatched shoes.

I followed Megan and Ringo across the chaotic room to an area with a sign that read: COSTUMES AND PROPS. Wasn't the whole crazy place covered in costumes and props?

"Check out the aquarium," Ringo said. He veered toward a windowed blue room that did resemble a fish tank. Inside were two prize fish: Anna Zafrani, the star of the show, wearing all black—except for the blue sunglasses hooked over the neck of her black shirt—and a taller girl with honey-colored hair, a willowy build and olive skin covered with layers of makeup. Both girls were reading from scripts, gesturing, making faces and generally overacting.

I guess I was staring at them with a confused look on my face, because Megan poked my shoulder and explained, "That's a rehearsal room. Anna and Jenna are working. We're supposed to leave them alone when they're working."

It was easy to interpret the slight whine in her voice: If Ringo or I screwed up rehearsal, Megan would lose valuable popularity points with Anna Zafrani and her costar, Jenna.

Inside the rehearsal room, Anna stopped reading. Eyes on Ringo, she stretched like a cat, then gracefully gathered her long black curls into a knot.

I bit back a grin. "Too late, Megan. It looks like Ringo's been spotted."

"Hey, who's that?" someone called out from behind me.

A sudden tapping on the glass of the outside windows made me jerk around with a fright. (I really have to lay off the sugary sodas.)

Three girls giggled, waving at the cute guy outside the window.

"Who *is* that?" Megan asked. I couldn't say anything since my jaw was on the floor.

"A dude," Ringo said, as if gorgeous guys appeared at classroom windows every day.

And he was an older dude, maybe sixteen or seventeen. Definitely in high school. He had dreamy sun-bleached hair that curled over the collar of his worn leather jacket. Long, dark lashes framed eyes that reminded me of shimmering green pools. He looked like the kind of crush you'd see in a motorcycle ad, riding off into the sunset on his Harley. But what was he doing *here*?

"AJ!" The girl with honey hair flew from Anna in the rehearsal room to greet the guy at the window. Jenna. As she ran toward the window, the guy's face lit up like a Christmas tree. She tugged the window open, then leaned out to kiss him.

I jumped as Megan elbowed me in the ribs. Okay. I was staring. You could say gaping. Something about that kiss was so cool. And so . . . old.

"You think that's Jenna's boyfriend?" Megan whispered.

"No, Megan. It's probably just one of the lawn maintenance guys," I said, rolling my eyes. Not that I wasn't a little thrown myself. I mean, Jenna was what? Maybe two years older than we were? Did things change that fast?

My thoughts raced. Jenna. Older boyfriend. "She must be that friend Toni talked about," I whispered to Megan. "Remember? Older boyfriend. Car?"

The guy was definitely crush material. But I couldn't believe someone from my school was seeing a high school kid. My brother, Billy, was sixteen. He'd gotten his driver's license a few months earlier. I tried to picture him dating someone from Trumbull. Car-obsessed meets the teddy-bear crowd. Too weird.

Over by the window, Jenna was just coming up for air. "What are you doing here?" she asked AJ, smoothing her hair over her eyes.

AJ held up two big paper bags that made my junk-food radar beep. "Special delivery," he said, pulling out a packet of french fries. "I remember the sawdust they call food around here. No one can live on that stuff. Besides, what's a rehearsal without the recommended daily allowance of grease and sugar?"

This guy was growing on me—and on everyone. Kids made for AJ like he was a magnet. Even the diva Anna. "You could have used the door," she purred, taking a bag of onion rings from AJ with long, slender fingers. What was her deal?

"Too easy," I heard him answer. "And the Trumbull authorities aren't too hot on graduates coming back to corrupt the inmates."

My mouth was watering for an onion ring, but I still had unfinished business with Megan. And she was holding back. She looked peeved, lips pressed into a tight line, as she was talking to a black girl with a shiny ponytail who was tacking a panel of heavy cardboard to the wall.

"Does this happen a lot, Stephie?" Megan asked. She took a tack from the girl and pinned it precisely on the corner of the panel. "What if Mr. DeLucca sees that guy? He doesn't even go to Trumbull."

The girl moved down the panel, pushing in tacks with a vengeance, more or less ignoring Megan's busybody language. "Yeah, well . . . I guess that's Jenna's problem. Doing the scenery is mine." I liked this girl. Stephie had spunk.

"Uh, right. I brought my friend Ringo to help us out." Hands on hips, Megan pivoted. It's not every day you see supergirl Megan at a loss for words.

"Megan," I said, holding up a hand. "We're not through. We need to talk."

But the words evaporated into thin air. Wasted. She was watching Ringo.

"Ringo. What are you doing!" she shrieked. She ran over to the rehearsal room, where Ringo was sharing Anna's onion rings. Megan was like some peasant apologizing to the local gentry as she grabbed Ringo and pulled him out of the room and over to Stephie.

My brown hightops tapped on the floor. How long was I supposed to wait? Why couldn't I get her to listen to me? "Megan?"

But she was setting up Ringo with a hammer. Not a good combo.

"This is so . . . swingable," Ringo said, swinging the hammer in wide, dangerous arcs.

"Ringo! Look out!" Stephie and Megan screamed in unison.

Too late. The hammer crashed into a can of orange paint, which toppled into two other cans and hit the floor with a loud dramatic thud. There was a major scramble as Stephie and Megan jumped to stop the domino effect, but the damage was done.

I cupped my hands over my mouth so Megan wouldn't see that I was about to explode from laughter.

Orange paint swarmed around Megan's black shoes, and she froze, not sure where to move. Ringo just stood near the mess, muttering, "Sorry, guys. It was totally an accident."

Funny as this was, I had hit the limit. "Megan . . ." I said, tracking her as she danced away from the puddle. "Listen to me. This is important."

"Tell me about it. My mother is going to kill me. Does this stuff wash out?"

I crossed my arms over my chest. "You know what I mean."

Megan sighed. "Okay, okay." She slipped off

her shoes and sat them on a square of newspaper. Then I motioned her toward a mirrored wall, away from curious ears. "What do you want me to do?" she asked.

"Level with me, for starters. Did you get any more letters from I KNOW HE CARES?" I asked.

"Casey Smith!" Indignation flashed in her eyes. "Weren't you just spouting off to Ms. Vermont about the right to keep a source confidential? As a reporter, I can't reveal *my* source. Period."

"But I'm a reporter, too," I shot back. "A reporter who's on the kid's side. A reporter who's going to write one whopping story about child abuse."

Megan hesitated. I could practically see her brain switch into editor gear. "Straight news, editorial or human interest?" she asked.

"Straight news," I answered, feeling a twinge of hope. "Information and statistics for kids our age. Warning signs. What we can do to help."

The story kind of mapped itself out in my head as I talked. I was *made* for this kind of juicy news.

Listening, Megan examined her shoes, making sure every speck of orange had been wiped off before she dropped the newspaper into the trash. "Could be a worthwhile story," she said thoughtfully.

"That's why I need your help," I said. I edged closer to ask persuasively, "Did you get any more letters from I KNOW HE CARES?"

"I emptied the box this morning," Megan answered. "But that is all I'm telling you, Casey."

"Then let me see the first note you got," I begged.

"No."

"Come on, Megan. You saw Chris at the Hole-in-the-Mall yesterday. I need to know whether he's the kid who wrote that letter. I need to get him on record."

"No again," Megan said, shaking her head. "Absolutely not. I mean, the story sounds good. But I'm not going to help you find out if it's Chris or anyone else. The last thing this kid needs is you on his or her case."

"You're so wrong," I snapped. "This kid needs a champion right now. This kid needs me."

"Back off the story, Casey." Megan folded her hands across the front of her neat red jumper. "You're going to scare away I KNOW HE CARES."

I couldn't believe what I was hearing. "Back off? You're talking to the wrong . . ." I broke off as something wet sprayed over me.

Dots of orange. And yellow.

Megan's jumper was splattered with yellow, too.

"Mustard?" I said aloud.

"Paint!" Megan said, swiping at her sleeve.

Paint was flying everywhere. And it was coming from . . .

"Ringo!" we all yelled at once.

Ringo was spinning in a circle, letting paint fly from the brushes in his hands. "Autumn! It's my abstract interpretation. Spontaneous seasons. Weeeeaaaah!"

Megan dropped her head into her hands. Bad move, considering all the paint that was on them.

Spontaneous Ringo was over the top. Too much for everything-in-its-place Megan. Enlisting Ringo was not one of her better ideas.

"Hey, Picasso," I said, grabbing Ringo by the shoulders to steady him. "If it's autumn . . . chill."

Is it art? Or a One-Burger-with-Everything-Hold-the-Burger?

Girl Escapes Green Cuisine!

TO: Wordpainter
FROM: Doctormom
Dear Casey,
At the risk of bugging you, I will. It's probably time to clean your room. Did you ever go shopping with Gram? Tell me you are *not* wearing that same old under-wear. And promise me you'll eat some-thing green for dinner, okay? That does *not* include pistachio ice cream!
Miss you like crazy. XXXOOO,
Mom

I laughed when I read the e-mail after school on Monday. Leave it to Mom to keep tabs on me from halfway around the world. She e-mails me at least three times a week. Sometimes three times a day.

The truth? I love getting those reminders. They make me feel like Mom is a lot closer than Southeast Asia. Like I can just run down the hall and talk to her.

I clicked on the icon to send a return e-mail:

Did you hide a videocam in my room before you left, Mom? Okay, I'll straighten up. Promise. Gram and I are going shopping this week. Really. And I'll work on the green cuisine. Just remember, good nutrition doesn't happen overnight.
Hugs to Dad and Billy.
Love, Casey
P.S. Do green M&M's count?

I caught myself with a goofy grin on my face as I clicked "send." It felt awesome to be home after such a news-sleuthing day. I kicked off my Converses, then flung myself onto the Chinese pillows covering my bed. My room is full of stuff my parents have brought me from places they've worked. Shadow puppets from Indonesia. Tibetan river stones. Striped Peruvian bedspread. The mounds of dirty clothes and old printouts were a design touch I had added myself.

My mom is always bugging me about my bomb of a room. Parents can be such a pain in the neck sometimes. But I appreciated mine more now that they were on the other side of the world.

That, plus I have a grandmother who dropped a happening reporter's life to stay with me. Well, she didn't drop it, exactly. She *was* writing her memoirs. But she left New York City to come to a sleepy town in the Berkshires just to be with *me*. How cool is that?

I don't normally get warm and fuzzy over my family. But when I thought about I KNOW HE CARES I realized how lucky I was.

What was it like at the end of the day when that kid headed home from school? Was it scary? Probably. Terrifying? Maybe. I rolled over, clutching a pillow, and watched the ceiling fan go round.

I wasn't about to back off my story. Megan couldn't stop me. I was going to help that kid.

I jumped up and went back to the computer to type in some keywords. For the next hour I zoned out doing research. You know how that is. I jumped from one Web site to another. Printed stuff. Soaked up facts.

An hour later, my desk was a mess of print-outs I had downloaded from the Net. By the time I called Megan, I had already copied some stats into my journal. Just the ammo I needed to blow away the Preppy Princess.

"Hello?"

"Hi, Megan. It's me," I said. "Listen. About my story on I KNOW HE CARES—"

"There *is* no story," Megan cut me off. "We already talked about that, Casey."

"We can't ignore this," I insisted. My printouts started spilling to the floor as I slid my journal closer to read the statistics out loud:

> "More than 3 million cases of child abuse are reported each year. . . .
>
> "In the overwhelming majority of cases, the abuser is someone the child knows, a family member or friend . . ."

I paused for effect.
I heard Megan draw in her breath. "Casey . . ."
But I wasn't done yet.

> "Nearly fifteen out of every one thousand kids in the U.S. are victims . . .
>
> "More than three kids die *each day* as a result of child abuse or neglect . . ."

I could almost hear Megan's brain trying to take it all in. "Wow" was all she said.

A direct hit. Score one for me.

"Now do you see why I have to find the kid at Trumbull?" I asked.

"I can't compromise that person's privacy. Period," Megan said.

I wasn't backing down. "Think about it, Megan. Three kids die *every day* from abuse. What if the next kid is someone *we know*? What if it's Chris? What if something bad happens because we backed down from this story?"

Megan's measured breathing came back at me over the line. "Maybe a story on abuse. Give the statistics. Make people aware," she said. "But only if you can relate it to Trumbull. *And* without compromising the privacy of JAM."

"One story, hold everything important, coming right up," I said sarcastically.

"Casey?" Gram's voice came from outside my door.

"Gotta go, Megan," I said, hanging up.

Gram was wearing yellow sweats, a T-shirt and her red-silk robe with the dragon embroidered on it. Her standard outfit for working at home. She was holding two long celery stalks.

"Your mother says green M&M's do *not* count," she said, handing me a celery stalk. "Personally, I think vegetables are underrated. They're great in Chinese dumplings. Grilled pepper heroes. Sundried tomato with linguine . . ."

My mouth began to water. "Pasta for dinner?" I asked hopefully.

"Grilled chicken from Chickaroo." She bit into a celery stalk. That's one of the other things I love about Gram. She's the takeout queen. Pizza. Chinese food. Meatball heroes. Gram doesn't spend a lot of time in the kitchen, but we never starve.

"Underwear shopping, day after tomorrow," Gram went on. "And try to do something with this room, okay? I have to report back to Parental HQ."

She was halfway out the door again, but I stopped her. "Gram? What do you know about child abuse?"

Gram turned to look at me with serious eyes. "Why?"

I spilled the story of I KNOW HE CARES. The letter. Megan's refusal to help me figure out who the kid was.

"That's a tough one," Gram said, chewing thoughtfully. "You want to help. And you also want to get the story."

"Which means I need to know who the kid is," I said with a big fat sigh.

Gram raised an eyebrow. "Even at the expense of someone's right to privacy?"

Just what Megan had said. Ouch. "Making sure that kid gets help is more important," I insisted.

"Careful, Casey," my grandmother warned. "You're walking in a mine field. Have you tried e-mailing a child abuse prevention organization to get some concrete advice?"

The doorbell rang.

"That'll be the Chickaroo delivery." Gram patted down the pockets of her robe. "Where did I leave my wallet?" She hurried down the hall.

I glanced at my computer. Gram had priceless answers. There was one last Web site to check. Kneeling on my chair, I clicked to get on the site and started scrolling through.

The site was set up in memory of kids who had been abused—kids who had died from abuse.

Name after name, photo after photo.

Most of the kids didn't even make it to the age of five.

I felt helpless. There was nothing I could do for Jaimie and Courtney and Ando and Tanya . . .

"But there *is* something I can do for other kids," I murmured, staring at the photo of a smiling little boy.

I clicked on the e-mail icon and wrote an urgent note that I had a "friend" who needed some advice.

I had the power of the word, right at my fingertips.

Still, at that exact moment, that power didn't make me feel a whole lot better.

Cartwheel King Jumps Gender Gap

DATELINE: Tuesday, lunchtime. Casey Smith in the gym with chicken sandwich and carrot sticks. File this one under: You've Got to Be Kidding.

"Someone else must have programmed my feet to come here," I said to Toni as we climbed up into the first row of gym bleachers with our lunches. "Someone with a sadistic streak and a sick sense of humor." I glanced down at the red hightops I had put on with my favorite jeans and black T-shirt. All of which were clean, thanks to Mom's e-mail nudging.

"I thought you were a newshound," Toni said as she sat down. The camera strapped around

73

her neck clunked against the bead necklaces looped over her neon-purple shirt. "Trumbull's first-ever male cheerleader at his first-ever practice? That's news, girl."

"It's enough to make me lose my lunch," I muttered. I was there because Ringo had asked me to come. Period.

Toni snapped off a few shots of Ringo down on the court, mingling with the other rah-rahs. I tuned out while they all lined up and did the shouting thing. But you know what? Once they split up and took turns doing flips and stuff, Ringo was like a one-boy show. The Human Cannonball. The High-Flying Pretzel. The Cartwheel King.

"You go, guy!" Toni whooped, as he came out of a handspring flip combo move, landing right in front of where we sat. "Are you sure one of your parents isn't a rubber band?"

Face flushed, Ringo stopped to catch his breath. "I don't think so," he answered. "My mom was in a band in the seventies, though. The Psychedelic Strings. She played the ukelele."

"Uh, Ringo? We've got to work on this free-association thing." I reached into my paper bag for my leftover Chickaroo-on-pita sandwich. "How about a quote for *Real News*? You're probably the only one on the squad who has the brain power to put together a complete sentence."

"Not true," Ringo said, bouncing down to do a few toe touches. "I've been doing some research. Did you know that eighty-seven percent of girls on our squad carry a B average or higher?"

I took a sip from my juice box to wash that surprising bit of info down. "Right. As if one statistic can wipe out the *huge* grossness factor here."

Toni's gaze sliced through me. "Let the boy make his point. Ringo, what else?"

"Stereotypes are lame," Ringo said. "Cheerleaders are brainless? Guys have to play football? I heard Marcy telling some of the girls I shouldn't even be on the squad."

I sized up the girl he nodded at. Long blond hair in a ponytail. Pink polo shirt. White lace anklets. "Marcy looks like she could use a good kick in the—"

"Casey . . ." Ringo looked over his shoulder. "You're not getting it. Well, whatever, dudettes. Gotta get back in formation."

While Ringo joined the line on the gym floor, I cracked open my journal to the notes I had written the night before:

How to find the identity of I KNOW HE CARES?

Raid Megan's files to find original letter. Is Chris I KNOW HE CARES? Talk to him! Talk to Gary!

"Do you know Chris Slater?" I asked, tapping my finger against the page.

"This free-association thing is catching." Toni lifted her camera as Ringo started stomping and shouting with the others. "You going to start making sense any time soon?"

I gave her the scoop. Showed her the JAM letter from I KNOW HE CARES. Told her about Chris.

"I tried to talk to Gary about it. I mean, he's on the football team with Chris," I said. "But Gary acted like I shoved a bee up his nose or something. He wouldn't even hear me out."

If Toni knew what was up with Gary, she wasn't saying. Her rings flashed as she put the lens cap on her camera. "So you don't actually *know* Chris is the one who wrote that letter," she pointed out. "Lots of kids get hurt, Casey. That doesn't mean their parents are beating on them. You need more to go on."

Did I mention that I hate it when other people are right?

Still, I couldn't let go. "But I *have* more to go on. My research. I found out that the abuser is usually a family member or friend. And you should have seen the way Chris's father was yelling at him."

Toni pulled her necklaces out with a finger, then let them shower back against her shirt. "Not enough to convict, Casey."

"If I could just talk to Chris. . . . Maybe he fits some kind of profile," I said, scouring my notes. "Wait . . . a profile. That's it!"

It wasn't until after school that I could really focus on the story. While Megan edited Gary's profile of the swim team at Dalmatian Station, I logged on to the computer and checked my e-mail. There was a message from that crisis center.

TO: Wordpainter
FROM: KidHelpers
We're so glad you contacted us. See if your friend exhibits any of the typical signs of abuse:
- injuries the person can't account for, or for which the explanations don't make sense
- withdrawal or sudden change in personality
- avoidance of friends
- changes in personality, eating, or sleeping habits

Please e-mail us again, Wordpainter. Your friend needs help.
—KH

These people didn't waste time. And neither should I.

"Now all I have to do is find out if Chris fits the profile," I murmured as I printed out the list and taped it into my journal.

"What did you say, Casey?" Megan straightened up from Gary's article, which was dotted with neat red editing marks.

Oops. I was so caught up that I forgot the JAM Police were there. I slammed my journal shut. "Nothing. Have you seen Gary?"

"Actually, he just stuck his head in the doorway a few minutes ago," Megan said, setting aside the story she'd been working on. "When he saw you, he must have changed his mind. He looked kind of mad."

"I must have forgotten to admire his new sneakers or something," I said, sort of worried. I hoped Gary got over himself soon. I needed his help getting to Chris.

With a few minutes to kill, I decided to spill my new story to Griffin. I clicked on the "mail" icon and typed:

To: Thebeast
From: Wordpainter

Hey, beast boy! I know you chose your name because a griffin is a beast, but have you checked your male dominance meter lately?

Speaking of males who rule, Ringo made alternate on the cheerleading squad. Whoopie! He's thrilled. I see major bleacher butt in my future.

But do I *have* to be supportive? Must I stand by while girls dipped in bath gel called "Only Iris" pat his arm and talk about scissor kicks? End of rant.

Back to the male dominance thing. I'm onto something big. . . .

I filled him in on the story of I KNOW HE CARES and clicked on the "send" icon. Maybe Griffin would have some ideas to help me identify this kid.

I checked the time, and groaned when I saw the tiny clock on the computer screen. "Just two hours until the game with Deergrass," I said, thinking out loud. "I must have been temporarily insane when I promised Ringo I'd be there."

"If I didn't have Drama Club, I'd go, too." Megan slid Gary's article into a folder and put it into the file drawer of one of the desks. "Night games are the best. I don't know why you're not excited about it."

"Football is about as thrilling as the prospect of bulking out on brussels sprouts. It's so . . . rough."

A tight smile wrapped around Megan's face, as if my words were germ cells and she needed to mobilize against them before they invaded her body. "I know Ringo appreciates your support," she said.

"Whatever." I was barely listening as we closed the newsroom and headed down the corridor. My mind was zipping ahead. There was just enough time for takeout Chinese with Gram, and . . .

"Hey, look." I paused at the front lobby, grabbing Megan's arm. "That's Chris."

I nodded toward the kid in the football jacket ahead of us, at the door leading outside. It was Chris, all right. His arm was still in a sling, which made it tough to hang on to his books while he maneuvered the door. The guy looked miserable.

"Casey," Megan warned. "You're not going to—"

Whatever she had to say, I didn't need to hear it. I was too busy jumping forward to grab the door and hold it open. "Hi, Chris! I'll get that. Actually, I was hoping we could talk . . ."

"I have to go," he mumbled.

I crouched down, trying to get him to look at me. No go. His eyes were glued to the scarred floor tiles. "Listen, about your shoulder—"

Talk about a weird expression. Chris looked at me as if I were a pit viper springing into attack. He started to take a step forward, but I held up my arm.

"Chris, I just need to talk to you for a minute—"

"I said I have to go." Pushing my arm away, he barreled past me and headed for a car that was waiting out front.

"Did you see that?" I said to Megan, as the car drove off.

"You were hounding him," Megan said sternly.

"Excuse me? Did I touch the guy?"

"You came on too strong," she said angrily.

"Correction. I should have come on stronger. Look." Letting my backpack drop to the floor, I rifled through until I found my journal. I held it out, pointing to the list I had printed from Kid Helpers. "He fits the profile, Megan. Injuries the kid can't account for . . . withdrawing from friends . . ."

"You don't even know him!"

Okay, maybe Chris and I aren't best buds or anything, but still . . .

"And didn't you say Chris told you how he

81

hurt his arm?" Megan continued. "Some accident at home or something?" Still steaming, she tapped a fingernail against my list. "And this thing about abused kids changing their habits? You don't know if Chris is acting different or not. Because you don't know him."

I grabbed my journal back. "There was something strange about the way he was acting just now. Didn't you see it? Something's up. I can feel it."

"All I see is that you're stretching the facts to build a story," she snapped.

I bit my lip. I was not—or was I?

"His excuse about his arm *could have* been bogus," I insisted. "And the way I saw his dad treat him . . ."

"You're way off base, Casey. Chris is not the kid who wrote that letter," Megan said. She stood like a rock, arms crossed over her blazer.

Then it hit me. "You know something!"

Megan's eyes jumped nervously to the driveway in front of the school. "There's my mom! See you tomorrow, Casey."

"Megan, you can't—"

Too late. She was gone.

Scientists Confirm:
Nachos Cure Adolescence

"I HAVE A theory about nachos," I said to Ringo that night as we shared a paper bowl dripping with hot cheese and salsa. "They can make *anything* more bearable."

I was sitting under the stadium lights at Deergrass Middle School, in the second row of bleachers. Ringo was right in front of me, a lone splash of red and white on the bench reserved for the cheerleaders. The rest of the squad was on the sidelines waving their pom-poms and shouting their little hearts out.

And silly me, I forgot my earplugs.

Boys bulked to the max in football gear clustered along the sidelines. From the field came the sound of groans and crashing helmets. And, quite possibly, hooves pawing the ground.

As I said, the nachos helped.

"Now I know how those packets of ketchup in the mall must feel," Ringo said as he reached back for another nacho. "It's ready. It's waiting. The guy with two double cheeseburgers reaches for the ketchup and . . ." His sneaker tapped incessantly as he gazed down the empty length of bench. "It's left behind. Wasted."

"Not wasted, Ringo," I corrected him. "If there was a big emergency right now. . . . Say Sahara broke a fingernail or lost her color-coordinated barrettes? You'd be in."

Ringo grinned as the girls on the squad made a kind of victory wave with their pom-poms, in response to what, I have no idea. There was no way I could watch the boys on the field charge into each other like rhinos.

He shot his own pom-poms up into the air as the wave of cheering people crested around us. I was the rock that sank to the bottom. At least Ringo didn't seem to notice my total immunity to school spirit. I didn't want to burst his bubble.

"Looking good, Ringo," one of the cheer-leaders called as the group broke their V-shaped formation.

Ringo brushed his hands off and turned to me. "What do you think of my uniform? Some of the girls thought I should go with a bodysuit. But

I think this is more my style."

I checked out the red-and-white Trumbull sweater with matching red sweats. Ridiculous to me, but then again a bodysuit sounded positively embarrassing. "Not bad, if you're into that kind of thing."

My mind shot back to my investigation as I found my target on the bench. Number 13. Chris Slater.

"Look," I said. "Coach Slater is so busy yelling at the players on the field, he can't spare a microbyte of attention for his own kid."

"Number thirteen," Ringo said, nodding at Chris's jersey. "That dude needs a new uniform. Bad luck and all that."

"His number isn't the problem, Ringo. His dad is," I said. "Or at least, that's what I've been going on. Now Megan says I'm way off. And I know she knows something."

I told Ringo about Megan's burst of information that afternoon. "I couldn't get her on the phone afterward, and now she's at school working on sets."

"Dead end," Ringo said, slightly preoccupied with the sideline spectacle.

"End of story." I sucked some cheese from my fingers and studied my stubby (and only slightly grimy) fingernails. Then I said: "If Chris isn't I KNOW

HE CARES, who is? It's like I have to start my whole investigation all over again."

"Isn't Gary supposed to be here?" Ringo asked.

I wiped my hands on my jeans and scanned the sidelines. Gary spent most games warming the bench and covering the play-by-play. But he wasn't around tonight.

"Missing in action," I said. "Megan's going to freak if he doesn't get the story. This is a game between rivals." Did that sports-talk really come out of my mouth?

Downfield blinding pops of light came from Toni's camera as she snapped pictures of the crowd. Then she turned to the cheerleaders and the action on the field.

I noticed that another photographer was roaming the sidelines with her. A taller girl with honey-brown hair.

"Isn't that Jenna?" I asked. Not that the image of her kissing AJ, the high school guy, wasn't a permanent part of my memory bank now. Weird.

Ringo nodded. "She and Anna were pretty cool about the paint yesterday. They let me help them rehearse their lines after I cleaned up."

Anna. Did Ringo have any idea that she was treating him like a lost puppy? I glanced over at him, but he was up and running. "Gotta jam," he called back at me as he headed for the huddled cheerleaders.

Toni snapped shots of Ringo's series of cart-wheels, then walked toward me, Jenna at her side. "Where's Gary?" Toni asked. "That boy's gonna have *me* to deal with if he doesn't get the story to go with my killer photos."

"You know how picky we paparazzi are," Jenna added as she plunked down next to Toni and me. She gave a dramatic toss of her hair, then held an imaginary camera my way. "Hey, Cinderella! You're beautiful, kid. They're gonna love you in *Teen People* magazine. Say *nacho*!"

"This is Casey, from the paper," Toni said to Jenna. To me, she added, "And this lunatic is my friend, Jenna Randazzo."

"Grin and say 'greasy cheeseburger,'" Jenna said, lowering her camera.

That was when I saw it. A faint bluish-black ring around her left eye. Makeup? She definitely had it caked on. I know I'm not exactly a cosmetics-counter expert, but that ring didn't strike me as a new trendy look.

"Jenna's just goofing around till her boyfriend shows up," Toni said.

"He didn't give you guys a ride?" I asked, remembering the scene with Mr. Baxter and his minor freak over Toni riding with a high schooler.

"His car got a flat, so Toni's mom drove us," Jenna said, smoothing her bangs over that ringed eye. She added happily, "AJ will be here before halftime, though. Made me promise to save him a seat at the top of the bleachers."

"Wait till you meet him, Casey," Toni said.

"Actually, I already—"

"He's the bomb," Toni steamrolled over me.

"How did *you* meet AJ?" I asked Jenna.

"You know how it is," Jenna said. "Girl goes on vacation with parents at lake. Girl crushes on gorgeous guy." She held the back of her hand up to her forehead and gave a dramatic sigh. "Total love at first sight. Cupid's big thunderbolt—"

"We get the picture, girl," Toni cut in.

Jenna laughed. "What can I say? The rest is romance history."

Okay, the girl was a ham. A likeable, melodramatic ham. She definitely acted to please the crowd, and we were pleased. Still, what was an eighth grader doing with Toni and me—puny peons from grade six?

"Is that a black eye?" I asked Jenna. I couldn't believe I actually said that out loud. I guess I still had injuries on the brain. My eyes kept flicking over to Chris, his arm in its sling sticking out like a chicken wing.

"This?" Jenna self-consciously tapped at her

eye, then grimaced. "Just my luck. I wound up on the wrong end of a field hockey stick on Friday. Don't you just hate sports?"

"Only the brutal ones," I said. This was a girl after my own heart. I was definitely warming up to Jenna Randazzo. "I always knew gym class was dangerous! It should be banned."

"Especially for klutzes like me," Jenna agreed. "I'm in the nurse's office so often, they've got a chair with my name on it."

A light blinked on inside my head. Duh! Nurse's office! That was the logical place for kids with injuries to go. Why hadn't I thought of it before?

I cracked open my journal and wrote discreetly, so that no one else could see:

Talk to school nurse. Try to match
student injuries to what I know about
I KNOW HE CARES. Find out if Chris has been
treated for injuries.

When I closed the cover again, Jenna was waving to someone in the distance. "AJ! Over here!" she yelled.

Toni and I both shot our heads around. I guess you could call it synchronized gaping. The newest sport at Trumbull.

It was AJ, all right. With a leather jacket and a killer smile that was aimed straight at Jenna. Somehow I managed to scrape my jaw off the ground before he reached us.

"Hey, Toni." AJ gave Toni this breezy wave before grabbing Jenna's hands and giving them a squeeze. "Hey, you. Miss me?"

I squirmed when they kissed. For once, I wished I *were* invisible. But I wasn't, because I suddenly felt AJ's huge green eyes turn toward me. "This is Toni's cool friend Casey," Jenna said, leaning into the crook of his arm and squeezing his hand.

"Cool Casey?" he teased.

Whoa! What do you know? I actually scored one of his knockout smiles. He obviously didn't know I still had a stuffed animal collection.

"You guys want something to drink?" he asked, nodding toward the concession stand and standing to leave. "The sugar rush is on me."

I wondered if my first boyfriend would be so awesomely concerned with my stomach.

Toni shook her head and her hair shimmered, as if it were trying to escape her tight ponytail. "No, thanks, babelicious. I need my hands to shoot."

"I'm okay, thanks," I added, squeezing my nacho bowl into a crumpled-up ball.

"I'll hook up with you later then, okay, Toni?" Jenna fell into step with AJ, talking over the sleeve of his jacket.

"Nice to meet you, Cool Casey," AJ called.

They were like a couple on a Valentine's card. Unreal. Definitely out of my league. Does getting past the sixth grade make you automatically cool?

Suddenly all the Trumbull fans were in a tizzy and yelling, "Touchdown! Touchdown!"

Toni bolted to the sidelines to shoot the action. "Later, Casey!"

I climbed down from the roaring bleachers and headed for the concession stand. All those waving arms and booming voices were starting to get to me. The way everyone was going crazy, you would think they had just won the lottery.

I definitely needed more nachos. Or maybe a chocolate fix.

I bought another order of nachos and made my way back through the chaos to the bleachers. I looked for the same spot in the second row where I had been sitting behind Ringo.

A man the size of Texas had filled in the gap.

"Casey."

I knew that voice. I knew the boy with that voice. Tyler McKenzie. He was sitting in the third row with two friends. He had actually spoken to me! Okay. Act cool.

"Um . . . hi, Tyler," I said as casually as I could.

"Would you mind?" Tyler gestured toward the football field. "You're kind of in the way."

Not exactly the romantic invite to sit with him that I was hoping for. "Oh. Yeah, sure." A couple of nachos spilled as I jumped out of the way. "Uh . . . see you," I mumbled, wiping cheese off the front of my jacket.

GIRL REPORTER LAUGHED OFF THE FIELD

I wanted to crawl inside the mountain of nachos and never come out. Casey Smith, the hermit of Nacho Hill.

I walked toward the sidelines where Ringo was sitting. Halfway there, I spotted Gary. Not in uniform. And on crutches.

A bandage was wrapped around his left foot and ankle. He struggled toward the bench. No easy job, considering the crowd and the muddy field.

Ringo saw Gary, too, and we both bolted right over to him.

"Gary, are you all right?" I asked. "What in the world happened?"

Gary winced as Ringo and I each took an

elbow and helped him to the bench. "It's just a sprain. No big deal," he said. "What did I miss, guys? I need highlights, names, scores . . ."

He flipped open his notebook, his eyes jumping from the players to the scoreboard.

"Baboons grunt. Run. Throw. Grunt. You know the drill," I said.

Gary glared at me. Whoa, man. Was he *still* mad at me? What had I done?

"Come on, Gary. I'm *kidding*," I said, fake punching him in the arm. "Did you sprain your sense of humor, too? Tell me what happened."

"I tripped on something at home," he snapped. "Do me a favor, will you, Casey?"

"Sure," I said. "Just as long as it doesn't involve muscles, sweat, helmets, scores or whatever else you like to call news."

Gary angled over one crutch to scowl at me. "Take a hike!"

Girl Reporter Hit by Asteroid

STUNNED, I BAILED to a safe distance, away from the battleground. And I don't mean the bruisers toughing it out on the football field. Gary was so mad that he didn't even want me near him. Thankfully, Ringo climbed up the bleachers to join me.

"What's eating Gary?" I asked him. I tried to sound cool, but I was really bummed and worried.

"You." Ringo reached for a now-cold nacho from the new order I had so far only managed to get on my clothes.

"But what did I *do*? Forget to worship at his Jocks Rule altar?"

Ringo shrugged. "Maybe it's how you constantly diss what's important to him. But I'd ask Gary."

That comment was so *un*Ringo. But I wasn't going near Gary any time soon. "Maybe he's having an allergic reaction to me. He wouldn't talk to me about Chris. His ankle—"

"Some people are very sensitive about their feet," Ringo put in, sounding more like himself.

"But Gary? Come on," I said. "He's not exactly Mr. Emotional."

"He is now," Ringo pointed out. "I guess even tough guys feel stuff."

He had tuned into something. "Gary *has* been different lately," I thought out loud. "He's been sort of sulky and withdrawn. Like yesterday. He got steamed at me for no reason and stormed out of the office. And now this. He's obviously upset, but he won't say how or why."

It all sounded familiar. Darkly, coldly familiar.

Handing over my nachos, I flipped my journal open and showed Ringo the list of typical signs of abuse. "Injuries the person can't account for; avoiding friends; sudden change in personality . . ." I read from the list. "That's Gary! What if I was wrong about Chris? What if *Gary* is I KNOW HE CARES?"

Ringo glanced at Gary on the bench as he crunched down on another salsa-covered triangle. "I don't know . . ."

But I was on a roll. "I said all the kids who

wrote in to JAM were losers," I went on. "No wonder Gary's so mad at me."

"You know what I've been thinking?" Ringo checked in on the squad before turning back to me with clear gray eyes.

"What?"

"Anyone could have written that letter to JAM," he said. "Gary. Chris. Anyone. But if it *is* Gary . . ." He stomped one foot, then the other, shaking crumbs from his sweats. "I seriously doubt he would tell you about it. Secrets are like satellites—"

A swarm of flies could have held a buzz-a-thon in my mouth right then, that's how wide it opened. "Wait! Why not?" I demanded, interrupting Ringo.

"News flash, Casey," Ringo said without looking at me. "You're not the most sensitive person in the world."

Ouch. When Ringo hits the nail on the head, he pounds.

"If Gary's in a bad situation, why would he tell *you* about it?" Ringo went on. "So he can see his life splashed all over the pages of *Real News*?"

REPORTER CALLED CALLOUS MORON BY FRIEND

"Hey, I can be just as sensitive as anyone," I argued. Somehow it didn't come out as forcefully as I'd intended. "I'm trying to *help* I KNOW HE CARES!"

Wasn't I?

Or was I just trying to get a story?

I stewed through the second half. Ringo hung near the cheerleaders. Tyler watched the game with his buds. Chris's dad kept ignoring him. Gary sat on the bench, waving a couple of players over for quotes. And Casey Smith gathered butt splinters.

When I couldn't take it anymore, I made myself go over to Gary.

"Want something from the concession stand? Power drink? Soda? Chocolate to help you remember how much you like me?" I asked.

But Gary wasn't signing any treaties. He shook his head and turned his face toward the field.

The Wall of Silence was up.

I looked away, and that's when I saw Jenna and AJ. A man was with them now. I couldn't hear what he was saying, but I could read the scene. Red face. Arms flailing.

Major tirade.

Jenna looked freaked. And AJ's arm was around her and it looked weird, like he was protecting her. But from what?

Something about the scene kept me watching. I snagged Toni by the arm as she angled her camera up for a shot of the crowd. "What's the deal with Jenna?" I asked, pointing.

Toni looked, then frowned. "Busted," she said, hoop earrings clanking as she glared at my hand, as if to say, Don't touch the merchandise. "Jenna's dad hates AJ. She's not even allowed to have a boyfriend until high school. She lied to get out of the house, but he obviously figured it out. Uh-oh. There goes my ride home."

I saw that Jenna had moved away from AJ. She followed her dad toward the parking lot, and AJ disappeared somewhere into the crowd.

"You can get a ride with Ringo and me," I told her. "His father won't mind."

Ringo's dad is a sculptor. At least, I *think* that's what he does. Whenever I get a ride with Ringo in their beat-up orange Volvo, his father's hands are covered with clay and paint.

"Thanks," Toni said. "I'll find you after the game." Then she was gone. Back to the sidelines to catch the next play.

I made my way to the edge of the field but stopped at the gate to the parking lot. Jenna and her dad were just getting into a car. In my mind I flashed on Jenna's black eye. Then on the rage I'd seen in her dad's face.

I remembered what Ringo had said about how I KNOW HE CARES could be anyone. Gary. Chris.

Or Jenna.

I mean, think about it. The girl had a black eye and an angry father. Very scary.

No reason to panic, I told myself. So Jenna's father was ticked off. She *did* lie to him. In my house a lie was grounds for, well, getting grounded. All parents are big on getting the truth. So when they hear a lie? Major downer.

But that didn't mean Jenna's father was going to hurt her, did it?

I swallowed hard as a car door slammed in the darkness. "I hope not," I whispered. "I really hope not."

Hockey Stick Modeled After Caveman's Club

YOU CAN IMAGINE how freaked I felt the next morning when Megan was nowhere to be found.

The girl had info I needed and she was dodging me big time. I was tempted to march over to her house and dig through her files myself. But breaking the law was a little beyond my safe zone. Besides, I don't think I could keep a clear head surrounded by all that pink decor.

Then I got a big break during gym class. I had somehow been pushed into playing field hockey, but Mindy Yang was pushing harder. Literally. The demon girl tore past me, just missing my face with her stick. But then. . .

"Oomph!" Her elbow found my stomach.

I doubled over and fell into the grass. Could someone please help me put my guts back in their original position? Talk about getting the wind knocked out.

I was ready to show Mindy Yang what it feels like to rub your nose in the grass when it hit me: This was a surefire way to get a crack at interviewing the school nurse. Griffin is *always* reminding me to see the bright side.

I winced, hamming it up as my gym teacher, Ms. Tickner, helped me off the field. "*Ooooh.* I need to go to the nurse's office," I acted. Forget the Pulitzer. This was an Oscar-worthy performance.

For someone who looks like Tinker Bell, Ms. Tickner can cut through the pixie dust pretty quick. "Just rest for a few minutes, Casey." She steered me toward a bench. "I'm sure you'll feel better."

I started to object. Until I saw the guy who was already sitting on the bench. Gary. He was twirling a soccer ball on one finger. His leg with the bandaged ankle stuck out like a bike kickstand.

I had forgotten that Gary had gym class the same time as me. My mind started churning out questions. What was the real deal with his ankle? Why was he acting so different lately?

"Hey, Gary, I—"

Something made me stop. Maybe it was the

set of Gary's jaw when he looked up and saw me. You would have thought it had been poured in concrete. If looks could kill, there would have been a chalk line around me.

So I just sat on the bench like an idiot with my hand over my aching stomach. What was the matter with me? Casey Smith is *not* one to back off a lead. Or anything.

You want the truth? I felt guilty. Ringo had laid it on strong the night before.

CARTOONIST BLASTS REPORTER

And if Gary was I KNOW HE CARES, my insensitive comments had made a bad situation worse.

Then, all of a sudden, Gary said, "What? No wisecracks? No third degree?" He stopped spinning the soccer ball and set it on the bench between us. "You must have really had the wind knocked out to cork you up."

I swallowed hard. All that pride didn't exactly go down easy. "Look, Gary. I'm sorry for whatever it is I did. And by the way, what'd I do?"

I saw a spark of interest in his eyes. "Could you speak up, Casey? I'm not sure I heard you right."

Oh, he was loving this.

I wanted to kick Ringo for that "Ms. Insensitive" speech. But I had to follow through.

"I'm sorry," I repeated, pumping up the volume a little. Although I still didn't know what I was sorry for. Maybe I really did need to sharpen my sensitivity radar.

Gary gave a nod, then reached for one of his crutches and used it to make a line in the packed earth around the bench. He didn't exactly jump up to congratulate me for being the Princess of Warm Fuzzies. But at least he wasn't spitting fire anymore.

"The thing is," I went on, "when I saw you last night with your ankle . . . did something happen at home, Gar? It's okay to talk about it."

It took him less than a millisecond to react. "I'll kill him!" he breathed, jabbing the end of his crutch into the ground.

I was definitely onto something.

"Is it . . . your father?" I asked, as gently as I could.

"No. *Ringo!*" Gary exclaimed. "He swore he wouldn't tell!"

My ears were burning. This was big. And scary. "Tell what? That your dad hurt you?" I probed. My heart was about to pound right out of my chest.

"What!" Gary looked at me like I just asked him to eat bird droppings. "I tripped over my cleats. Why would you think *my dad* hurt me?"

Talk about confused. Now I felt like we were

each on our own planet. "That letter in JAM. . . . Someone wrote about getting hit . . ."

"And you thought it was *me*?" Gary cut in, letting his crutch fall to the ground. "Are you out of your mind! My dad would never do anything like that!"

"But . . . you were so mad at me. Acting as if you're allergic or something. And abused kids back off from friends . . ."

Gary shifted his hurt foot so he could turn toward me. "So you decided my dad was beating on me? You don't even know him! Did you ever occur to you that the reason I was mad was because of something *you* did? Like bulldozing over my story about pressure in sports?"

"Pressure in sports?" It seemed like ages since I had even thought about that story. I had to do a major mental archeological dig to get back down to it.

"Oh, puh-leaze, Casey," Gary ranted. "Your angle was a total ripoff of mine. That really ticked me off. You totally thought you could redo the story, only better."

GIRL REPORTER BUSTS SPORTSWRITER'S EGO

He had a point. More than one.

I knew I had to admit my mistake. "Sorry, Gar,"

I told him. "About your dad. The story. I was off the mark. I didn't mean to step on your toes, so to speak."

Was this the new Casey Smith talking? The *sensitive* Casey? I could barely stand myself.

"Anyway, I should've told you I decided to drop that story after I found out someone here at Trumbull was being abused," I explained. "I know it's not you now, but what about Chris Slater?"

Annoyance pinched his face again. "Strike two. You're way off base with Chris, too," he told me.

"Just hear me out." With that ankle, at least he had to sit and listen to me.

I presented the evidence. The way I'd seen Coach Slater treat Chris. The shoulder he hurt at home. The stuff on abused kids from my research.

Gary just kept shaking his head. "Casey, I was *with* Chris when he hurt his shoulder," he told me. "He did it when he was pulling his mountain bike out of the garage. Coach Slater wasn't even home."

Ever watch a balloon fly around and flap to the ground after someone lets go of the tip? Well, that was me, Casey Smith, Sensitive Reporter, with her two biggest leads shrinking to nothing.

Suddenly Ms. Tickner was standing in front of us. "Feeling better, Casey?" she asked.

"Not really," I muttered, turning on the actress juice. This was my big chance. My only chance now that Gary and Chris had alibis, so to speak. Hand on my stomach, I doubled forward and groaned. "I *really* need the nurse."

Footnote: She had to believe me, because what kid wants to go to the nurse? Get real.

She clutched her whistle. Tinker Bell was a tough sell. But I had been elbowed in the gut.

Five minutes later, I was walking into the nurse's sanitized office with a note from Ms. Tickner in my hand. Drama queen Anna Zafrani herself would be impressed.

The place was a cold-comfort zone. Sparkling metal table. An eye examining station. Bandages and medicine in a locked glass case. Oxygen tanks. Posters with a pyramid of food groups on the wall. I had never noticed before that cows are more or less in three out of four basic groups. My stomach started talking to me, but it wasn't pain. I wondered if Gram was in the mood for burgers tonight . . .

"I'll be right with you," Ms. Maresca, the nurse, told me. She was tending to a girl with the nastiest knee scrape since that time Griffin bit the dust blading down his front steps. The hefty nurse blocked my view, but I saw short braids, the light-brown skin of the girl's arms and the bandage the nurse was putting on her knee.

"The swelling ought to go down in a day or two," Ms. Maresca told her. "In the meantime, I suggest you keep away from field hockey."

"How about banning field hockey altogether?" I said, as I put Ms. Tickner's note down on the desk. "It's not a sport. It's a brutal method of torture."

Hmm. A future editorial?

Note to self: Logic? If you hit a kid with a stick in math class, you get expelled. So why is it okay during gym?

"Another casualty?" asked Ms. Maresca. She was large and jolly, with round, pink cheeks. Picture a young Mrs. Claus.

"From Ms. Tickner's class," I answered.

As the nurse turned to smile at me, I got a better look at the girl she was treating. It was Stephie, the girl who had been working on the scenery for Drama Club. She tapped the bandage on her knee, then moved to another chair.

"Sit and rest a few minutes, honey," the nurse told her.

"But I'm missing my science class," she protested.

"I'll write you a note. I don't want you rushing around right now, dear. Now, let's see . . ."

The nurse picked up a clipboard and slowly copied my name from the hall pass. No hurry here. I definitely didn't want to rush back to Tinker Bell's hockey torture.

"So tell me," I said, trying to remember my list of questions, "what's the most common injury kids come in with?"

"You're looking at it," she replied, pointing to Stephie's knee. "Cuts, bumps and bruises. Usually from contact sports in gym class."

A good start. But I needed more. "What about accidents that happen outside of school?" I asked. "Do kids come to you with those?"

"Sure. Sometimes," she said, preoccupied with her paperwork.

"There must be some kids who are accident-prone," I pressed. "You know, kids who are always turning up with something or another. I bet you could tell a lot of stories. What kinds of explanations do they give?"

"Oh, you know. This and that. Everybody has a story," she said as she took my pulse.

"You must hear some real whoppers," I went on, thinking I was majorly sly. "Like . . . what, for example? My turtle bit me? My tongue got caught on the ice-cube tray? What's the best story you ever heard?"

Ms. Maresca blinked, raising a warning eyebrow at me. "Casey . . . that kind of information is confidential. What are you up to?"

I gave her my best "Who, me?" look. "I'm doing a human-interest piece for *Real News*. On the walking wounded here at Trumbull." It was kind of true. "Kids like me, and Stephie . . ."

Stephie smiled at me as she pulled up her gym socks.

"And Jenna Randazzo."

I watched the nurse for her reaction. But Stephie was the one who paused.

"You know Jenna?" she asked me.

"Sure. Enough to know that she's a total klutz," I said. "I saw that fierce black eye she got during field hockey on Friday."

"Wait." Stephie frowned. "Jenna's in my gym class," she said. The short braids on her head swayed as she shook her head. "And she wasn't hurt in class. She didn't even show up for class on Friday."

Reporter Charged with First-Degree Nosiness

I RAN FROM the nurse's office and found Gary outside the locker rooms after gym. "Emergency meeting," I told him. "Lunch period. Newsroom. Can you find Megan? I'll get Toni and Ringo."

Gary nodded. I guess he could see I meant business. "What's up?" he asked.

"No time. I'll tell you when we meet, okay?"

My last class before lunch was social studies. I swear someone pressed the slow-motion button. Ms. Hernandez droned on endlessly about Congress and the President. How a bill becomes a law. How a bill gets vetoed. Normally I'm totally down with politics and Capitol Hill. But today I just wanted to get to my own summit meeting.

I felt like I'd aged years, but finally the bell rang. Freedom. I ran to the phones outside the administration office and called Toni's pager to leave a message. Then I scanned the halls looking for Ringo.

Normally we met each other in the cafeteria. But today I had a feeling he wouldn't be there. Trusting my instincts, I hightailed it to the drama department.

There were a dozen kids in the room. And then there was Anna. She had this yellow turban thing wrapped around her hair, and she was practicing in the rehearsal room. Was she running lines alone?

Just then a pair of arms shot into the air in front of her. Arms in the shape of a V for victory.

"Yes! You nailed it!"

I knew that voice.

I stepped up to the doorway as Ringo added, "That was great, Anna. Totally medieval!" He was sitting beneath the window in his baggy overalls while Anna stood soaking up his praise.

"Ringo?" I called from the doorway. "Did you hear about the meeting?"

He pushed up off his hands, springing to his Birkenstocks. "What meeting?"

"That's a no. It starts in two minutes. You *have* to be there." Grabbing Ringo's hand, I pulled him from the room.

"Thanks, Ringo!" Anna called. "See you at rehearsal after school?"

I couldn't believe it when Ringo flipped her a thumbs-up sign over his shoulder. "Def," he promised.

"As if she doesn't already have enough people tripping over themselves to impress her," I muttered. "Now she needs her own personal cheerleader?"

Ringo shrugged, tucking his spiral notebook under one arm. "I've been running lines with her. Anna says I really help without breaking her concentration."

BOY CHEERLEADER DROPS REPORTER FOR DRAMA DIVA

"You've got to keep your priorities straight, Ringo. Don't let that egomaniac start taking up all your time."

"Egomaniac?" Ringo whistled through his teeth. "That's harsh."

"Okay, fine. Whatever. Look, Ringo, right now I want to talk about the paper. The news. The stuff that happens in the real world. Not that pseudo-drama dimension Anna lives in."

I was walking and talking in high gear. Ringo started doing one of his cheerleader skips to keep up with me. "I guess a pseudo dimension is a kind of alternate," he said. "Alternate on the squad. Or an alternate kind of guy . . ."

"Ringo, don't go loopy on me. Just tell me you're not trading *Real News* for Drama Club. Seriously, do you have any Simon cartoons ready for our next edition?"

"Yeperdoo," he chirped as we cruised into the newspaper office. The place was a morgue. I dumped my books on Dalmatian Station and frowned. "Where is everyone?"

"The cartoon dude is right in here." Ringo flipped open the cover of his notebook. "And I've got more in the files. I already scanned copies of two new Simon 'toons."

One Simon for every day of the week . . . ?

Ringo did a cool side step to the desk that held all the newspaper files, pulled open the top drawer and began flipping through the folders.

"Here." He grabbed a folder and plunked it down in front of me.

Since no one was in the office yet, I decided to take a breather and see what Ringo had Simon doing in his latest cartoon. I opened the folder, but what I saw wasn't a cartoon. It was a pile of handwritten letters—JAM letters!

"Oh, my gosh!" I breathed. I always figured Megan locked them away at home. "Ringo! These are JAM letters. The *originals*!"

"Whoa, backspace," Ringo warned. "I must have grabbed the wrong folder. Megan doesn't want anyone going through that stuff. It's confidential. Secret Service. CIA."

I heard what he was saying, but I wasn't listening. I started reading through the pile, checking the signatures. "Ignored . . . Painfully Shy . . ."

"Score!" My heart thumped wildly when I found I KNOW HE CARES. Pulling the letter out carefully, I held it up like it was burning my fingers.

"What do you know. The letter lives."

"Yeah?" Ringo leaned closer, his gray eyes thoughtful. Who was just bugging about Megan's warnings? "What does it say?"

The note was written on white paper. Pretty basic, except for the cute little gray mouse at the top right-hand corner. The one that floated up on pink, heart-shaped balloons.

"Pink!" I crowed. "Whoever wrote this *has* to be a girl."

"What's the deal with pink?" Ringo said with a hint of irk in his voice. "Why do guys take one look at that color and it's see yuh! Totally excluded from the male world."

I examined the letter. The handwriting had lots of flowery loops. And there were a few stars drawn in the margins. This was definitely not written by Gary or Chris. . . .

"Girls don't think twice about wearing boy colors, like blue or black," Ringo went on. "Why can't—"

"Casey!" Megan's shout cut Ringo short.

Uh-oh. Busted.

Megan stood in the doorway. Her cheeks red, her shoulders stiff. How long had she been there? "That file is confidential and you *know* that! How dare you snoop!"

"It was an accident! Sort of," I struggled. "Ringo was getting the Simon cartoons out and pulled it out by mistake. It just kind of . . . happened."

"Oh, sure." She reached around me, grabbed the letter from my hand and quickly closed the JAM folder. "Do you really expect me to believe the letter *fell* into your hands by accident? You've been stalking me for that thing all week."

Ringo rubbed his thumb and forefinger together in front of Megan's face. "These fingers are the guilty parties," he said, explaining the details in Ringo-speak.

"Besides," I said, "I was going to find out the truth, one way or the other. You can't throw out bait the way you did yesterday and not expect me to bite."

Megan just stared at me. Was I winning her over?

GIRL REPORTER ACQUITTED ON TECHNICALITY!

"You *wanted* to tell me it was a girl yesterday," I persisted. "But you chickened out at the last minute."

She bit her lip and folded her arms, like she was hugging the JAM file. "I just hated the way you badgered Chris. It wasn't right."

"Okay, I admit I was clueless about Chris Slater," I said. "But I've got a new theory."

Just then Toni strode in, and Gary hobbled on his crutches behind her.

"What's with the big emergency meeting?" Gary said, propping his crutches against a desk.

"I need help with my story," I said.

Toni frowned. "Are you telling me that I gave up time in the darkroom for that news flash?" She slouched against one of the desks, arms crossed over her T-shirt and drawstring cargo pants.

"You mean the story about the abused kid?" Gary asked, carefully maneuvering into a chair at Dalmatian Station.

I took a deep breath. "Look, it's more than a story. I want to find out who the kid is so we can help her."

"Her?" Toni said. She sat down at the table next to Gary.

"Definitely. Come on, Megan. Hand it over." Reluctantly, Megan held up the note with the cute little mouse and swirly handwriting. "I think I know who it is, too."

Even Megan was hooked. I could see it in her perfect blue eyes. "Who?" she asked.

"Well," I began, my eyes avoiding Toni, "Jenna Randazzo has a black eye. She supposedly got it playing field hockey on Friday. Except I happen to know that's a lie. She wasn't even in gym that day. That's where I need your help, Toni," I said, finally looking at her. "Do you know how Jenna *really* hurt her eye?"

Toni's amber eyes burned into me like lasers. "You think *Jenna* is I KNOW HE CARES? Have you totally lost it, girl?"

Remember that advice about staying on Toni's good side?

"It *could* be her," I replied sheepishly. "That's all I'm saying. Didn't you see how mad her dad looked at the Deergrass game last night? And what's the story with her mother? Maybe she's the one . . ."

"Her mother is *dead*, Casey Smith. And you are so wrong." Toni stood, heaving her backpack on her shoulder. "Do you think I'm here to get grilled by you? Or for you to tell me my friend is a human punching bag?"

"No, Toni, wait . . ." I protested. "I'm just trying to—"

"Save it!" Toni snapped. "You know what? I don't need this. I'm outta here."

No one said a word as Toni shot out the door. A second later she doubled back, pausing in the doorway. "Don't you ever try that again, Casey." She whipped her hair back and jabbed her finger at me. "Don't *ever* trick me into backstabbing a friend."

And then she was gone.

Girl Reporter Skids Over Trapdoor

"TONI, WAIT!" MEGAN called after her.

Ringo leaned out the door to eyeball the hall. "Gone," he said.

"Casey has that effect on people," Gary said. "Has anyone else noticed?"

"Excuse me?" I glared at him. "This isn't about me. It's about this girl. What about the rest of you? Are you going to help?"

"I'm in," Ringo said.

Gary picked at the rubber pads of his crutches before nodding. "Me, too. Just promise you won't hound Chris or me anymore."

"Deal." I turned to Megan. She was the wild card here. "Well?"

Megan sat there with her hands neatly folded

in her lap. She looked so . . . thoughtful. So mom-like. It was enough to make you want to check to make sure you didn't have eye boogers or something.

Finally, she spoke. "I've read more than a dozen letters from kids about I KNOW HE CARES," she said thoughtfully. "They want to help. They want to know more about abuse and what they can do. People are really concerned. Sure, privacy is still an issue, but . . . I want to help, too. This is important."

"You're saying you *want* me to do this story?" I asked.

"I'm *saying* we should help this girl," Megan said quickly. "And, yes, we need to do a story, but not before we figure out our next move."

She had a point. Leave it to Megan.

"But if we can help I KNOW HE CARES, I think we should." She took a deep breath, then added, "I think we have to. But that doesn't mean exposing a very personal problem on the front page of *Real News.*"

Megan and I were actually bonding? Break-through. Hold the presses.

"Okay, here's a plan." I opened my journal, writing down ideas as they came to me. "Megan, you know Jenna from the Drama Club, right?"

Megan nodded. "I can ask around. She's been

a member since her first year here. Maybe other kids in the club know something."

"I can help with that," Ringo offered. "I'll beam up to the drama dimension after cheerleading practice." He turned to Gary. "Will you be at practice to do my story?"

"Do I have a choice?" Gary poked his crutches at the gross gray linoleum, frowning. "When are you going to wise up, Ringo? Guys should *not* take orders from girls. Case closed."

"Oh, really?" Megan piped up.

Gary regrouped and tried again. "It's not even like these girls are jocks," he went on. "They're just . . . cheerleaders."

Ringo looked up from the doodle he was sketching in his notebook. "You're wrong. I got this cool book about cheerleading from the library . . ."

Uh-oh. Ringo was zigzagging along his own dimension now. "Focus. Jenna is the topic here, remember?" I reminded everyone.

But Ringo streaked ahead. "According to my book, sixty-two percent of cheerleaders are involved in a second sport," he said proudly. "And eighty-three percent are leaders in student organizations. And here's a serious stat: Cheerleaders suffer more injuries than kids in any other sport because of the extreme gymnastics they're expected to perform. What do you say to that?"

"We'll have a parade for the squad real soon," I said. I jabbed at the notes in my journal. "*After* we get the real deal on Jenna."

"What about her boyfriend?" Megan asked. "He's so crazy about her. Shouldn't we talk to him?"

I nodded. "Maybe he has a take on Jenna's dad. Or maybe he can get Jenna to open up. Talk about what's happening at home."

"He seemed nice," Megan said. "But how? Like we're really going to get a high school guy to listen to us."

Good point. But again, I had already thought of an alternate plan. "Isn't one of your brothers in high school, Gar?" I asked.

"Two of them, actually." After a moment, he caved. "I'll find out if they can get the four-one-one from AJ."

I wanted to keep cranking on the story, but the bell rang. As we headed out at the end of lunch period, my ears were ringing. Maybe it was my body reacting to the fact that I had actually munched the celery sticks in my lunch. Veggie rush? Get real.

"My story is finally happening," I told Ringo. I crouched down to tie the lace of my purple Converse while he dug in his locker. "Jeez! At last I'm getting somewhere."

"But too bad Toni's so bummed," he said.

"She'll get over it," I said. "Especially if it turns out that her friend really does need help."

"Another 'if,'" Ringo said. "Your stories always start with ifs. Very shaky ground. I'll stick to cartoons."

"Later," I said, turning toward Ms. Strader's class. His words stuck in my mind. Was I on shaky ground? Was this sure feeling an illusion? Was the whole abuse story a trapdoor that could open under my feet at any moment?

Don't even go there.

Hurricane Toni
Strikes Coast

THE NEXT FORTY minutes passed in a blur. Maybe it was a gift from the heavens, but Ms. Strader showed a film to kick off the unit on violent weather in science class. Lights off. I didn't even have to pretend to pay attention.

Besides, the footage of hurricanes, floods, blizzards and cyclones was nothing compared to the human tornado I found when I got out of class.

Hurricane Toni, headed my way.

"You have *got* to see this!" she shouted down the hall to me.

Megan hurried alongside her, her backpack hanging from one arm. "I'm going to be late for Mr. Baxter's class," she complained. "And I still have to drop off a layout for the Yearbook."

"What's up, guys?" I asked.

Megan just shrugged.

"I cannot *believe* she lied to me," Toni said, hands and hair flying all over the place. "How could I have been so stupid? I have been so clueless! How could she do that?"

She was talking a mile a minute. Something white flashed in her hand, but I didn't dare get close to see what it was.

Yikes. You'd think forty minutes was enough time for a chill pill to set in.

"Toni," Megan said, "tell us what—"

"I trusted her! She's supposed to be my best friend," Toni went on. "This whole time she's been lying. Not just about the black eye, either. Last month she had a sprained ankle, and a bruise on her arm, and . . . Wow. I just believed her made-up excuses. How blind could I get? And not only that, why wouldn't she trust me? All this time he was . . ."

"Toni!" I grabbed her shoulders and jerked her around to look at me. Not a smart maneuver under ordinary circumstances, but this wasn't ordinary. Not by a long shot.

Toni stopped, breathless. She blinked and wiped her nose on her sleeve. "I just found this in my locker," she said, handing me a note.

Hey, Girl! Want to go to a really wild party
with AJ and me tomorrow night? A big blast
out at the lake. I know you do. Just need a way
to get it past your parents. Call you later.
        Jenna

Right away, I knew it wasn't what the note said
that was important. It was what the note was
written on. Precious white stationery with a little
mouse floating up on pink, heart-shaped balloons.

Whoa. That clinched it.

"You were right, Casey," Toni said. "Jenna is
definitely I KNOW HE CARES."

Totally Useless Reporter Kicks Egg Yolks

"WE HAVE TO talk to Jenna," I said. "ASAP."

Toni nodded. "She's rehearsing for *Collages* this afternoon. I can't wait to get in her face and see what she has to say for herself. I'm ready to . . ."

"Hold on a sec," Megan said with her forehead scrunched. I knew what that meant: Megan's ever-faithful voice of reason was about to be heard. "You don't want to clobber the girl. This isn't about you, Toni. It's about Jenna. Put yourself in her shoes. She's being hurt. She's scared— of everyone. Why else would she write an *anonymous* letter to JAM?"

If it wasn't for her pink fetish, Megan might actually be perfect.

Toni twisted the rings on her fingers for a long

minute, then looked up and slowly said, "I didn't think of it that way." She rubbed her temples with both hands and closed her eyes. "Oh, poor Jenna. She doesn't deserve to be yelled at. She deserves my help. Our help."

"Okay, then," I said. "Let's go talk to her, Toni."

"You?" Megan raised an eyebrow at me. "You'll scare her socks off."

"I can be sensitive." Hadn't I just turned over a new leaf? Casey Smith, Sensitive Reporter. Protector of secrets. Supporter of cheerleaders.

"Jenna has met Casey," Toni said. "She likes her. Calls her Cool Casey."

"If you say so," Megan said. "But be mellow, Casey. Please."

"It's settled then. Meet me backstage after school," Toni ordered.

"And don't mention the JAM letter," Megan added. "I mean, we don't want her to feel like she's been trapped. Just try to get her to talk. In the meantime, I'll find Mr. Baxter. I think we need a teacher on this."

Once again, Megan was right. Abuse is a way bigger deal than stolen tests or coaches who'll do anything to win.

It figured that Ms. Belsky would choose the last two minutes of Spanish class to assign major homework. El groano. I had to stay late to copy down the info.

By the time I got to the door marked BACKSTAGE at the drama department, Toni was waiting. She had a look on her face I'd never seen before.

"This is scary," she said. Her hands worked frantically, adjusting the star-shaped ornaments that were braided into her hair.

Toni, nervous? This was a first.

"Don't worry," I said. "Ready?"

"No. But let's go," she answered.

We walked through the door practically holding our breath. Backstage was hopping, as usual. Megan stood with Stephie and a few other kids beside a huge piece of scenery. She nodded as we walked by.

That must mean Mr. Baxter agreed that talking to Jenna was a good first move. Not that it helped much. I still felt like we were walking into a pit of green slime.

Toni and I found Jenna clowning with some kids in the wings. They were trying on wigs and accessories from a costume box. Jenna was giggling and hamming like she didn't have a worry in the world.

"Hey, chicklets!" Jenna called to us. "What's up?" She wrapped a yellow feather boa around her neck and did some quick dance steps. "Just

129

getting ready to shoot a video for my new song. 'Feathers on Fire.'" Then she pointed the boa at Toni. "D'you get my note?"

"Yeah. But, um, we need to talk, Jenna," Toni said. She glared at the other kids standing around. "In private."

We headed for an empty part of the wings. Jenna paused in front of one of the heavy red curtains and looked back and forth between Toni and me. "If it's about the party . . ."

"It's about you, Jenna," Toni said, looking at her without blinking. "We're worried about you." For once, her sharp attitude was gone. Now I heard sincerity.

"I know, I know," Jenna admitted. "I'm totally stressed. With *Collages* and everything, I've gotten way behind in my homework."

"It's not about school, either," Toni said with a sigh. She took Jenna's hand and cupped it between both of her own. "It's about how you keep getting hurt. Girl, I know you haven't been telling me the truth."

Jenna's easygoing smile faltered, and she pulled her hand away from Toni's. "Wh-what are you talking about?"

"The black eye?" I reminded her. Then, remembering Megan's advice, I said as gently as I could, "That didn't happen during gym. You didn't even go to gym class on Friday. Please, Jenna. Tell us what really happened."

"It . . . was an accident!" Jenna backed up a few steps.

"What about that sprained ankle you had a couple weeks ago? And that big bruise on your arm? No one is *that* accident-prone, girl," Toni said, her voice wobbling. Was it my imagination, or was Toni the Tiger about to cry?

Jenna had a panicked look in her eyes. Major fear. I suddenly wished there was a teacher with us. Or Ms. Vermont, the counselor. Why hadn't I e-mailed Kid Helpers back?

"We can help you," I said. "You don't have to be afraid anymore."

"I—I don't need help." Her head shook back and forth in about a kazillion nos that made her honey-brown hair fly. Was Jenna trying to convince us? Or herself?

"Come on, Jenna," Toni pressed. "Trust me. Please."

Tears squeezed out of the corners of Jenna's eyes. "What do you want me to say?" she asked in a miserable voice. "That he hits me? What good will that do?"

She buried her face in her hands, sobbing. Heavy duty. I wanted to hug her really tight and tell her everything was going to be all right. But I just looked at Toni and mouthed a silent "Help!"

"Hey, I'm your best friend, remember?" Toni slipped an arm around Jenna's shoulders. "Why didn't you tell me? If your father's hitting you, the problem is his—not yours."

Jenna's head jerked up. She stared at us with wide, wet eyes. "It's . . . it's not what you think," she insisted.

Time for a reality check. "It's okay to admit that your dad did that, Jenna. It's not your fault."

She began to sob harder.

"I love him so much!" she cried in between sobs. "And I know he loves me. I just . . . I just want him to stop hitting me."

"You can't do this on your own," Toni said, tucking Jenna's bangs behind her ears. "You need real help. *He* needs help."

"What about Ms. Vermont?" I suggested. "That's what she's here for."

Jenna shook her head. "No! He'll get in trouble. They'll take him away!" She shivered, hugging herself. "I couldn't stand that."

I caught the look Toni shot my way. Total disbelief. "There are people out there who know how to deal with this stuff," she told Jenna. "And you don't know for sure that they'd separate you and your dad."

Suddenly, Jenna straightened up and wiped

her cheeks. "Look, I can take care of myself," she said, sniffling. "And it's none of your business anyway."

Toni said, "None of my busin—"

"Hey, Jenna! Where are you?" a voice called from the other side of the curtains. "We're rehearsing your sketch first."

We all sort of jumped.

"Be right there," Jenna called back. She wiped her cheeks again, trying to pull herself together.

"Wait!" I stepped in front of her, blocking her path. I wanted to stop the action and rewind so we could try again.

Except this time we would get it *right*. "Jenna, you need help. We're not going to go away because this problem isn't going to go away."

Tears glimmered in her eyes. Along with a desperate look. "You really want to help? Then don't tell *anyone* about this. Not a word. Promise?"

Before I could say anything, Toni spoke up. "Sure, okay."

"Thanks." Jenna flashed us a relieved smile. Then she stepped past me and disappeared in the wings.

"Nice move," I told Toni. "There's no way we can keep that promise. Jenna's dad is going to keep hurting her. We have to tell Ms. Vermont. Or call Kid Helpers. Or . . . something."

Star beads whipped around Toni's neck as she swung her attitude toward me. "We can't freak her out with guidance counselors who'll want to examine her from head to toe," she insisted. "Right now she needs us to listen and be good friends."

Maybe. But I felt like dirt.

Toni stuck around to update Megan and Ringo. I had to head home. I'd been dreading underwear shopping. Putting it off for weeks. Gee, I wonder why? Do you know anyone who actually *likes* browsing through the undies section? And now, after everything with Jenna, I was definitely not in the mood.

But Gram was waiting.

"Give me two minutes to finish this chapter for Nancy," Gram said, sticking her head out of her room after I walked in the front door. Nancy is a big shot in New York who's editing Gram's book.

"Take your time, Gram." A few years would be fine with me. "Doesn't the Underwear Connection have a Web site? Maybe we don't have to go to the mall."

Gram's red dragon robe swirled around her legs as she turned back to me. "You already tried on-line shopping, remember? Giant orange boxer shorts are not what your mother has in mind."

"Those boxers rule!" I said, fist in the air. "So what if they're a little big. They're killer to sleep in." I headed for the stairs.

"Those things would be roomy on an elephant." Gram disappeared back into her room, but her voice floated out to me. "No more excuses, Casey. We leave in ten minutes."

I trudged up to my room and logged on to the Internet. Not for shopping, though. Gram doesn't lay down the law very often, but when she does it pays to play the good citizen.

Ten minutes gave me just enough time to e-mail Griffin.

Surprise, surprise. There was already an e-mail from him waiting in my mailbox:

To: Wordpainter
From: Thebeast
Re: Yin/Yang
    Whoa, Casey. Child abuse is heavy duty. I know you're a pit bull when you're on a story, but what if there's more going on than meets the eye (no pun intended)? Are you sure you want to keep pushing this kid? For a story? We've all got our dark side—the yin to the yang. But that doesn't mean everything is

black and white. Remember Gram's speech about the gray stuff. It's key.

And speaking of stuff: Wassup with Ringo? Is that a jealous Casey vibe I smell seeping through cyberspace?

I stared at the words for a minute before clicking to write a return e-mail:

To: Thebeast
From: Wordpainter
Re: my so-called life
I don't get jealous, wise guy.

Okay, maybe I do. But if you could only see the way he kneels at Anna's feet like a panting puppy. She throws him a bone and he gobbles it up. A painful sight.

Hey, guess what? I found I KNOW HE CARES.

The bad news? Couldn't convince her to get help. Which means the abuse isn't going to stop. Scary, huh? And I hear what you're saying about the gray zone. But this story is too enormous for me to toss away. I want kids to get *real* info. But I don't want to hurt people in the process. Is that possible?

You know what? Scratch the Pulitzer campaign. Just . . . scratch.

Signing off,

TURKEY

(Totally Useless Reporter Kicks Egg Yolks)

Girl Reporter Enters "Most Mortifying Moments" Contest

"I AM *NOT* looking forward to this," I said to Gram as we walked through the Abbington Mall a half hour later. I was preoccupied with thoughts of Jenna, so everything reminded me of my non-story. Neon signs glowed all over the food arcade, and every one of them seemed to blink a personal announcement about me:

GIRL REPORTER FAILS. AGAIN. AGAIN.

"Has to be done," Gram said. "Don't you want to put an end to those nagging e-mail reminders from your mother? I know I do. Oh look, there's Clothes Barn."

"Sounds like the right place for a turkey," I mumbled.

Gram gave me a sideways look. "That bad?"

"Worse."

I gave Gram the rundown of what happened with Jenna. "I can't believe she actually turned down our help. Gram, do you think I should tell the school counselor even if it means breaking Jenna's trust?"

"I know Jenna's reaction is hard to make sense of," Gram said, dodging a woman with a double stroller. "But going against someone you love can be very difficult. Your friend just isn't ready to make that choice. As for the school counselor, you definitely need to—"

"Hey! Look out!" Two boys darted between me and Gram, obviously in the middle of some game of hide-and-seek. As immature as it looked, it was a whole lot better than trying on training bras. Ugh!

Gram steered me into the Clothes Barn and glanced up one long aisle. "Uh-oh. Never trust a store that's larger than a theme park."

We tracked down the girls' intimate apparel section. "I hate those names. Intimates? As if socks and underwear are best friends you'd share secrets with. And those fluorescent lights? You might as well just put a spotlight on me and announce: Heads up! Casey Smith is in aisle three buying underwear!"

"Crab." Gram had stopped next to a rack of shiny panties with flowers printed on them and looked at me.

I shook my head, and we moved on. "Okay, my story is getting to me," I admitted. "It's under my skin. A kid should be safe at home. Period. And you didn't finish telling me what I should do about Ms. Vermont."

"I will, I will. Let's just get you some new skivvies before the store closes." Gram held up a pair of kneesocks with black-and-white zebra-type stripes. "Look at these. Just like some I had back in the seventies. Op art was big back then."

She was trying to divert me, but I wasn't taking the bait. "I can't imagine not having somewhere safe where I can hole up and veg out and be me without worrying about anything."

I headed for a rack that caught my eye. Nothing shiny. Negative on the hearts and flowers. Just plain ole panties.

"You know," Gram spoke up from behind me, "it's only in the last few years that people have taken child abuse seriously. People often doubted kids who came forward."

I flipped through a rack of basic white cotton. Undies and undershirts. "But are things better now?"

"Better, but not great," Gram said, coming up

beside me with our empty shopping basket. "Even if authorities confirm abuse, the solution isn't always rosy. You say her mother is dead? Then your friend could be placed in foster care. Or she might have to move to another town to live with relatives."

Did Griffin call this one, or what? Gram was talking about the gray areas. The messy complications.

I hate gray.

Why can't things be clear and simple? Good or bad? Black or white?

"So you think it's right to try to help this girl?"

"I agree that you shouldn't back off."

I tried to focus on the rack in front of me. Do French-cut undies come from France? And how do people actually wear those skimpy things? Wedgie Central! "But what's the answer, Gram?" I asked, thinking aloud. "She said she couldn't stand being separated from her dad. But anything is better than staying in a situation where she's being hurt, right?"

"Absolutely. Something has to be done," Gram said. She tackled a bin of socks, picking out some in different colors. "This is a question of trust, Casey. That's why I want you to talk to Ms. Vermont first thing in the morning. It's time to get some professionals involved."

I thought about that while I grabbed the socks from Gram and threw them into our basket. Who cares what colors she picked out? I never matched, anyway. "The thing is, I'm a reporter. If talking to Jenna isn't helping, maybe I can write a story that will help."

"You want to expose her?" Gram shifted the basket to her other arm. She looked really serious. "Casey, that kind of bombshell can backfire. I don't want you in any compromising positions. Her dad could be dangerous. I mean this."

"But maybe it could help. Shock Jenna into doing something."

I kept looking through the rack. Okay. I was avoiding Gram's eyes. The eyes burning into me with an I'm-older-and-wiser-and-you-should-listen-to-me look.

Then, a sigh. "Do you want me to talk to the school counselor?" Gram asked.

I flashed on Toni's promise to Jenna. A promise was a promise. Still . . . if it only protected Jenna's father, what was the point?

"Um . . . no," I said, still unsure. "Jenna already knows I know. If you talk to Ms. Vermont she'll think I posted her problem on the Net."

"Okay. But if you change your mind, the offer is still on the table." Gram nodded at the pile of underwear I was still contemplating. "Well?"

I checked out the selection. White. Cotton. No ruffled edges. No special design. Undies with a satin edge I figured I could live with. What can I say? Some decisions are easier than others.

I grabbed as much underwear as I could and headed for the cashier. And I would've made it, too, if my biggest nightmare didn't become reality that exact second.

"Sure, Mr. McKenzie," a chipper salesgirl cooed. "We'll order the straight-cut jeans for you tomorrow."

Mr. McKenzie? As in Tyler McKenzie's dad?

Tyler had to be close by.

"If you'll just fill in your phone number right here . . ."

Tyler. Me. Assorted undies!

I ducked behind a rack of ugly raincoats, right next to a rack of ugly sweatshirts. Who knew I'd be joining those dopey boys in their game of hide-and-seek?

"Casey, is that you?" I knew that voice. "Why are you hanging out down there with all that stuff?"

I jerked around. The eyes confirmed what the ears suspected. I wanted to die! But first, I silently thanked the universe for its exquisite timing.

"Uh, hi, Tyler. I just, um, dropped these, um . . . socks," I said a little too loudly as I held up a package.

"Those aren't socks, Casey," he said, grinning as he turned and walked toward his dad.

I looked at my hand. Undies! I just waved a package of undies in Tyler McKenzie's face.

Oh, wake me up when this nightmare is over. . . .

CHAPTER
17

Real Bonds Begin in Bunny School

THURSDAY IS USUALLY pretty crazy for the *Real News* staff.

It's the deadline for getting stories in so we can rewrite, edit, do layout and get *Real News* in shape to go to the printer on Friday.

Picture all that, plus trying to help Jenna. And me with a story I knew was going to cause major shock waves.

Our lunchtime meeting kicked into overdrive practically before we got there.

"Okay, guys," I said, plunking my lunch and my journal down on Dalmatian Station. Chairs scraped as the other kids gathered around and took out their own lunches. My story about I KNOW HE CARES was burning a hole in my journal. But first . . .

"The subject is Jenna. Megan, any luck?"

I was momentarily derailed when I spotted the perfect creases running down the legs of her overalls. I mean, who irons overalls?

"Sort of," Megan said. She consulted a page of notes that was neatly centered on her clipboard. "I found two eighth-grade girls in Drama Club who were good friends with Jenna Randazzo last year. Laura Bruder and Tori Capella. They've both noticed a change."

"Details . . ." I probed. "What kind of change?" My mouth started watering as I unwrapped my killer ham and cheese with roasted peppers and pickles sandwich.

"Apparently, Jenna wasn't such a klutz last year," Megan explained.

I looked up, tapping my pen. "Are you sure? I mean, everything I've read says child abuse usually starts at a much younger age." I thought of the kids who hadn't even made it to age four. "This has probably been going on for years."

"Anna gave me the same rap," Ringo said.

"She talked to you? You're not even in the Drama Club," Megan said. I didn't miss the jealous cloud that darkened her blue eyes.

It almost made Ringo's defection to those drama heads worthwhile.

"Get over it, Megan," Toni said. "You're the one

who asked him to help out. Anything else, Ringo?"

His hair fell across his forehead as he nodded. "I talked to Stephie, too. She's known Jenna since they were, like, munching animal crackers together in bunny school."

"Bunny school?" Gary echoed, rolling his eyes. "You're hopeless, man."

"It was a Montessori bunny school," said Ringo, as if that explained everything. He went on. "Stephie gave me the same rundown. She says Jenna didn't become safety-challenged until this year. Right about the time she dropped Stephie as a friend."

Megan nodded, snapping her fingers. "That's what the girls I talked with said, too. Jenna's definitely been pulling away from them this year. Before that, everything was okay."

Toni stepped in. "She hasn't been dodging me." She paused, then added, "But we weren't close friends last year."

"I don't get it." I tapped my pen against my journal, thinking out loud. "It doesn't fit the profile. I mean, is there something we're missing? Some reason Jenna's dad would suddenly turn into a monster this year?"

"I don't know much about him," Toni admitted. "And now . . . Well, Jenna is definitely protecting him. When I called her last night, the girl went out of her way to tell me everything was okay at home. I don't know what to believe anymore."

"She still doesn't want help?" I guessed.

Toni's hair did its quivering thing as she shook her head. "Said she wished she'd never admitted anything. And that she's really glad we promised not to get her in trouble."

"Uuughh!" I growled at Toni. "I never promised. *You* promised for both of us."

Toni shrugged, fingering the bangle bracelets that covered her forearm.

"Jenna's already in trouble," Gary pointed out. "My brother Brandon wouldn't even talk to that guy AJ."

"Why?" Megan asked. "He doesn't know him."

"He knows him." Gary tilted his chair onto the two back legs, holding onto the table for balance. "Brandon says AJ is a loser. Apparently the guy is obsessed with his car. That and hanging out with younger kids."

I was kind of relieved to hear I wasn't the only one who thought that was weird. "Like Jenna," I supplied.

"Yeah. He hung out with some other eighth grader before her. Some girl named Melissa," Gary said.

"So what if he hangs out with younger girls?"

Toni's bracelets clanked as she twisted the ends of her hair in her fingers. "Nothing wrong with that."

"Maybe there is, Toni. Brandon said there were rumors." Gary let his chair come back to all fours, then propped up his injured foot. I couldn't help but notice that there was something brewing under that baseball cap.

"What kinds of rumors?" I demanded.

Gary took a breath and dropped the bombshell.

"He says AJ used to hit Melissa."

Eighteen-Wheeler Crashes Into Newsroom

I FELT AS if a Mack truck had just barreled over me with all eighteen wheels. "What?"

Megan's charm bracelet clinked delicately against the polka-dotted table as she leaned forward. "Gary, are you sure? I mean, if AJ is the one who—"

"Sorry I'm late, everyone!" Mr. Baxter announced from the doorway.

Talk about a conversation stopper. All of a sudden, the *Real News* room got real quiet.

And Mr. Baxter smelled the conspiracy. "Okay," he said, looking from one silent face to another. "What happened now?"

"Mr. Baxter." Megan shot him one of her I'm-in-control looks. "We may have been wrong about Jenna's dad."

Megan quickly unclipped her page of notes on Jenna and handed it to Mr. Baxter. "We think it's her boyfriend," she said calmly.

Mr. Baxter read the notes, then glanced from Megan to me. "This is the kid with the car, right?"

We all nodded.

Looking at Toni, he added, "You know, I was bothered by him from the get-go."

Toni just crossed her arms and stared at him.

"You all realize that I have to report this to Ms. Vermont, and she'll likely take immediate action."

"But—" Toni piped up.

"No buts," Mr. Baxter said. "You did a great job uncovering the truth, but now it's time for professional help."

We all just sat there looking at him.

"Okay then." He swung a desk chair over to Dalmatian Station. "Let's get this meeting rolling."

Meeting?

How could I concentrate on *Real News*?

That was a first. Usually I live and breathe and eat the news. But today my thoughts bounced all over while the staff discussed other features. Toni passed around photos that I couldn't focus on. Megan mentioned something about a new batch of JAM questions and answers.

Jenna's boyfriend had a reputation for being violent, I thought. For hitting his girlfriend! And

Jenna's injuries had started . . . when? After the summer. After she had started dating AJ. Why hadn't I put that together before! I had assumed it was Jenna's father who was hitting her. But now—

"Casey?" Megan's voice broke into my consciousness.

I blinked. Everyone was looking at me. As if they were waiting for me to talk. Obviously, I had missed something. "Yeah?"

"Your story?" Megan reminded me. "What's the status?"

"I've got a draft right here," I said, trying to pull the shades down over my worries about Jenna.

It wasn't until I had already handed Megan a copy of my story that I realized I'd blown it. Big time. Written a story about a kid whose *father* hit her. Pointed the finger at an innocent dad when it was really the no-good loser boyfriend who was the monster.

REPORTER'S SHODDY RESEARCH SENDS INNOCENT MAN TO DEATH ROW!

"Wait. Give it back, Megan. I need to do a rewrite . . ."

I made a grab for Megan's copy, but she pulled it out of reach. "Let's get input first."

"Megan, don't—"

But she was already reading the headline out loud: "'He doesn't mean to hurt me—When . . .'" She faltered for a second before picking up on the rest of it. "'. . . When parents hit their kids.'"

Mr. Baxter didn't seem to notice the looks that ricocheted between Megan, Toni, Gary, Ringo and me.

"This may be premature, Casey," he said, unwrapping his lunch. His hero looked like it was loaded with every cold cut known to man—and maybe a few that weren't. "But let's hear what you've got."

I waited for Megan to humiliate me. Read the story out loud and point out the major flaw in my guesswork. Not that I needed to hear what I'd written. I had combed over the words about a trillion times already:

> It happens to over 3 million kids every year.
>
> Some kids think they have no choice. It feels like there's no way out. Many kids blame themselves. And most kids are afraid to talk about it.
>
> They're afraid to tell people about it. That someone they know

is hitting them. Hurting them.
Beating them.

Three *million* kids every year.
Bruised. Burned. Or worse.

And by whom? The people who
should be protecting them. Their
parents.

You think it couldn't happen to
anyone *you* know. But guess what?
It can. It is.

The piece went on to tell Jenna's story. But I didn't use her real name, of course. Still, I'd supplied all the relevant details.

Or, as it turned out, all the irrelevant details. Now that it was clear that Jenna's boyfriend was the one abusing her, I was kind of freaked. I mean, how had I let myself jump to that kind of conclusion?

"Sounds like a good editorial on child abuse," Mr. Baxter said. "But until someone talks to Jenna's dad, I don't want a story on abuse splashed across the front page."

"Editorial?" I echoed. Looking at his puffy cheeks, I got the feeling they had just absorbed all the fat from his hero. "But what about the front page?"

Baxter looked at me in that I'm-the-authority-here way. I was the investigative reporter here. Everyone knew that. But at the moment, I had about as much of a front-page story as the gerbils in the science lab.

"We're going with Gary's write-up on Ringo as the lead article," Megan said, making a few notations on her clipboard. "The first-ever boy cheerleader at Trumbull."

"Oh. Right." Gary was a little slow on the uptake. He pulled some papers from his backpack and grimaced as he slid the story across Dalmatian Station to Megan. "Does my name have to go on it? I have a reputation to protect, you know."

"I'm going to be on the front page?" Ringo waded through the mist to join the rest of us. "Pictures and everything?"

Toni pointed a bright-red nail at one of the photos in front of her. "I got a great shot of that flying-pike thing you did at practice the other day."

"What about our regular sports page?" Mr. Baxter asked.

"We've already got the rewrite of Gary's swim team profile on disk," Megan cut in, consulting her clipboard. "What about coverage of the football game against Deergrass?"

"I've got it, but . . ." Gary frowned as he flattened

the two folded pages that remained in front of him. "It's a little light on details of the first half. I was hoping you could help me out, Casey."

"Me?" I flipped back in my journal to my notes from the game. Observations of Chris Slater and his dad. AJ. Jenna's dad . . . "I was focusing on the *interesting* stuff. Which means I've got exactly zero details on the game."

Gary threw up his hands. "Didn't anyone pay attention to the game?"

"Okay, get this," Toni said. Her bracelets cascaded down her forearms as she framed in an imaginary viewing screen. "Two minutes into the first quarter. Cal Pillson recovers after a Deergrass fumble, makes a death-defying leap around the Deergrass fullback, then doubles back down the line fifty-seven yards for the touchdown."

"Whoa," Gary murmured. "I missed that?"

"Then the Deergrass quarterback comes back with a killer pass straight up the middle," Toni went on. "We're talking greased lightning. Good for twenty yards. Deergrass thought they'd broken through. Then their receiver hits our wall. The Big Beef."

"Scott Hamburger!" Gary's fist shot into the air. "Trumbull's defensive linebacker. This is good stuff, Toni," he said, nodding. "If you write it up, I can—"

"Nuh-uh. I don't do the writing thing," Toni cut in. "I mean, I'll talk you through it, Gary. But don't press it."

"Just get together and get the article to Megan before the end of the day," Mr. Baxter interrupted, sparing us all a play-by-play snore-a-thon. "Ringo? How's Simon doing?"

Ringo brushed his hair off his forehead, then took a stack of comics from his spiral notebook. "Here's the thing. I've been wishing that Simon could be more cubelike."

Mr. Baxter paused with his can of soda halfway to his lips. "Cubelike?"

"All those different sides," Ringo said, crunching down on a cucumber stick from his lunch. "Each one is a little different, but they're all part of the same cube."

"Hello?" Gary waved a hand in front of Ringo's face, as if trying to wake him from a trance. "Does this have *anything* to do with *Real News*?"

Ringo stared at the pile of cartoons on the table. It was as if he were trying to identify a strange insect he'd been watching. "I mean, which Simon do I draw? The one who digs jumping into a herkie? Or the dude who likes the rush of boosting the fans' energy? The dude who can run faster than the players on the field?"

"Isn't it all the same guy?" Megan asked.

"I don't know." Ringo frowned. "Is Simon less of a guy because he hangs with girls? And likes some of the things girls like?"

Wow. I didn't realize Ringo was so freaked out about this cheerleading thing.

"It's just tradition, man," Gary said. "Guys play ball. Girls are cheerleaders. Don't take it personally."

"But the first cheerleaders were guys," Ringo countered. "So tradition can change, right?"

Megan stared at one of the cartoons. "It's your call, Ringo. Can Simon be a dude and still cheer on the squad?"

"I think so," he said, looking at Megan as if she'd just solved the biggest dilemma of his life.

"Then don't worry about it." She shot him one of her I-am-so-supportive smiles. Barf!

Mr. Baxter shifted restlessly, and we pressed on to the stories Megan was doing.

She'd written one story on the differences between street makeup and stage makeup. Another profile on Anna Zafrani, entitled "Diva of the Drama Department." And an editorial on the problems of treating child abuse.

That was three articles that would have her name on them. Plus JAM. Megan had been busy, all right.

"And we've slated page two for your coverage of *Collages*," Mr. Baxter added.

Ouch. Make that four bylines for Megan.

PERKY EDITOR WINS NEWSPAPER JOUSTING CONTEST

Okay, it wasn't supposed to be a competition. But I was going to have what? Just one byline in this week's edition? Maybe none at all.

This was bad. Very, very bad.

"Actually, I can't cover the production," Megan said. "It wouldn't be objective, since I'm going to be in *Collages*."

Gary stopped readjusting the Ace bandage on his ankle and looked up at her in surprise. "I thought you were just doing scenery."

"I was, but . . . well, Ellen Bruzelius is out with the flu, and Mr. DeLucca asked me to take her place," Megan explained.

"You're in?" Toni let out a whoop. "Excellent!"

Megan's cheeks turned pink as Gary and Ringo gave her high fives. To look at them all, you would think Megan had just been offered a chance to paddle up *Dawson's Creek*.

"Casey can do the write-up," Mr. Baxter said. "Any problem with that?"

I shook my head. Hey, it was a byline. Of

course, there was a downside. I would have to sit through the show.

I didn't waste too many brain cells worrying about it, though. I had other things on my mind. Like Jenna. And getting the real story on her and AJ so my only byline wasn't a fluff piece on the drama scene.

I needed to talk to Jenna. When I couldn't find her at any of her usual hangouts, I went straight to Ms. Kiegel, manager and chief know-it-all of the administration office.

"Mr. DeLucca sent me from the drama department," I said. It was a lie. But it was for a good cause. "He's worried that Jenna Randazzo didn't show for rehearsal today. For *Collages*. Did she go home sick?"

"Let's see." Ms. Kiegel reached for one of the stand-up files on her desk. The sacred stack. No one else goes near them.

Let me explain something about Ms. Kiegel. There's a sign on her desk that says it all:

> I CAN ONLY HELP ONE PERSON A DAY.
> TODAY IS NOT YOUR DAY.
> TOMORROW DOESN'T LOOK GOOD, EITHER.

So, what were my chances of pulling a fast one on Sergeant Kiegel?

"Hmm." She frowned. "Tell Mr. DeLucca that Jenna is on the absent list," she said. "He should call her father to find out if she'll make it for the show tonight."

Score.

"Jenna didn't come to school today," I told Ringo and Toni when I ran into them in the hall before our last class. "You don't think . . ."

"AJ?" Ringo filled in.

Toni reached into the pocket of the baggy jeans she wore that came to just below her belly button. "I'm calling her house. Maybe she just faked sick. Chilling before her big number in *Collages* tonight. Maybe she didn't spend the day with that mold-sucking lizard boy."

"I can't believe we all fell for his act," I said, scrambling to keep up with Toni as she made for the phones near the administration office. "Jenna painted a really great picture of the guy. And when I met him . . . he seemed nice. Cute. Junk food in hand. No signs that he breathed fire."

"Or hit girls," Ringo added.

I was playing it off, but it scared me that Jenna wasn't in school. While Toni pumped change into the pay phone, I tried to figure the possible scenarios. Jenna, hanging at home before her big night onstage, like Toni had said. But if not—

"Jenna! You're there!" Toni said into the receiver. Relief spilled all over her voice and face. "Girl, you had me worried. Is AJ there?"

Toni listened, then smiled and shook her head at Ringo and me. We could relax. The loser boyfriend wasn't around.

"Listen, I just wanted to wish you good luck tonight," Toni went on, absently hooking a finger around one of her belt loops. "Let's hang out afterward, okay?"

Lifting the heel of my purple Converse against the wall, I waited for Toni to hang up.

"Well?" I asked. "Why didn't you tell her we know about AJ?"

Toni planted both hands on her hips. "And totally freak her out? Are you crazy?"

Maybe. But not crazy enough to contradict Toni.

"We can talk to her in person," Toni said. "Tonight, after *Collages*. You know Jenna. She loves putting on a good show. She wouldn't miss this one for the world."

CHAPTER 19

Sneezing Tree Steals Show

"WHERE *IS* SHE?" I mumbled under my breath.

I circled backstage like a heat-seeking missile that hadn't yet found its target. Ten minutes to curtain, and Jenna was a no-show.

Not that it was easy to find anything or anyone back there. We're talking total chaos. Kids with clipboards barked out last-minute changes. One girl held pins in her mouth as she sewed kids into their costumes. Performers complained about itchy makeup. Techies dressed in black goofed around with props.

And Toni was everywhere at once, getting backstage photos for *Real News*.

"Have you seen her?" I asked, coming up behind Toni like a pouncing cat.

Toni shook her head, then angled her camera

163

up to get a shot of Ringo, who was one of four kids rolling scenery into the wings. He jumped over a fake bush and joined us.

"I can't find Jenna anywhere," I said, almost whispering.

"Mr. DeLucca is having a heart attack," Ringo told us. "He phoned her house, but no one's there. I was with Anna when he called an emergency meeting with all the actors. They're trying to figure out an alternate plan."

He nodded toward the rehearsal room. Stepping closer, I could see the drama advisor inside. He was surrounded by kids in leotards. Giant fruits and flowers bobbed above them— headdresses. Add to that a handful of girls in medieval dresses, and a wandering robot. I gotta admit it was cool in a bizarro kind of way.

"What is this? King Arthur Meets Star Wars? Or the Dance of the Food Pyramid?" I dumped my jacket onto a mountain of stuff in a corner backstage. The stage lights were up, roasting the entire area.

Toni shrugged. "Four sketches. Four themes. Four sets of costumes. It's called *Collages*, remember? At least Megan looks cool."

"If you like that Princess Leia sort of thing." Decked out like a princess, Megan was one big haze of white gauze and sparkles. Her blond hair was braided and coiled on her head, topped by a crown that glittered with fake diamonds. "Talk about typecasting," I said.

"Down, girl." Toni's face looked troubled as she scanned the stage. "Megan's so worried about Jenna that she's sure she's going to blow her lines."

"Maybe Jenna's just running late," Ringo suggested.

"She said she would be here!" Toni tapped her boot against the floor as she checked her watch.

"Ringo," called a girl with a daisy bouncing on her head. "Anna wants to see you."

Ringo dashed away as Toni peeled off to snap a few shots of the makeup crew touching up the green arms of a human tree.

I glanced down at the notes in my journal. Not the quotes from the cast, or the production notes I'd gotten from Mr. DeLucca. My eyes were drawn to the info I got on the phone from Kid Helpers that afternoon:

Statistics on Dating Violence

• More than one out of four teenagers experiences physical violence at the hands of someone they date.

• Teenagers may not look to adults for support.

- Victims may think abusive behavior is a normal expression of love.

I wanted Jenna to know she wasn't alone. That this had happened to other kids. That there were people who could help her.

I wanted one more chance to talk to her.

"Okay, it's show time, kids!" Mr. DeLucca's stage whisper broke my thoughts like a boulder dropping into a swimming pool.

I made a run for the auditorium, where the house lights were blinking. Not that I was such a show biz nut, but a reviewer ought to see the show. And Jenna could still make it. No need to panic.

Yet.

The curtain rose just as I grabbed a program and found a seat near the aisle, about halfway back.

SKETCH NUMBER ONE:
Spring. Interpretive Dance.

Half a dozen kids were onstage, frozen in awkward poses. Were they trees? Frozen Neanderthals? Bears waking from hibernation? Did I really have to suffer through this?

I was jotting down a few notes when a tree sneezed.

"Gesundheit," I said as a boy flopped down in the empty seat next to me.

Whoa. Not just any boy. Tyler McKenzie.

I could feel my cheeks get hot. I mean, why *that* seat? Did he *want* to sit next to me? Or was it the only empty seat he could find in the dark auditorium?

Should I say hi? Talk about socks? Pretend I didn't notice he was there? *What?*

GIRL REPORTER CHOKES

Sometimes I really wished human beings came equipped with instruction manuals.

"Check out the Kellehers," Tyler said.

Was he actually talking to *me*? I chanced a look and . . . major miracle. He was all mine. Dark eyes. Crooked grin. The guy had a look that could melt chocolate.

Did I mention that it was hot in there?

"Did you ever figure out how to tell the K-twins apart?" he whispered.

"I gave up trying back in third grade," I told him. "I mean, Kelly . . . Kalinda . . . Karma. What are their first names, anyway?" I pretended to look it up in the program.

We had both gone to grammar school with the K-twins, two girls with identical heart-shaped faces and blond ponytails. And if they had personalities, they were well hidden beneath their twin mold. At the moment, the Kellehers were on-stage in identical green leotards sprouting gauzy leaves. From identical twins to identical plants. What a stretch.

"Look, they're moving in perfect sync," Tyler whispered back. "At least with each other."

I held back a laugh when I saw the Kellehers twirling in the opposite direction from the rest of the vegetation onstage.

Time for the poison pen to fly. Tempting. But I guess I wasn't here to fry anyone. The point was to write a review that was honest *and* fun to read.

For now, I scribbled notes:

Sneezing tree. High energy. A few heavy steppers. Who knew leotards came in so many colors?

Polite applause peppered the auditorium as the curtain closed.

"What's next?" Tyler whispered.

I checked the program: "Summer of Discontent."

"With Annie Zee-Fanny." Tyler rolled his eyes. "She thinks she's a big deal because she had a modeling gig. For the Mackie's Hardware sale flyer. Woo-hoo."

"Really?" There was one Anna Zafrani rumor I hadn't heard. But when you're as hugely popular as that girl, a million stories swirl around you.

The curtain swished open to reveal Anna and a boy dressed in medieval costume.

"There she is," Tyler whispered, "Queen of Hardware."

"I didn't recognize her without her glasses on her shirt," I said.

We both laughed quietly, and I wondered just a little why Tyler was being so nice to me.

Anna's satin gown swept across the stage as she moved. Anna filled the spotlight. She filled the *room*. She had this way of reaching out and grabbing the audience. I made a note.

Anna Z. Stage presence.

"I know there's another world beyond these castle walls," she said, gazing into the spotlight. She sort of made me believe there were mountains and gardens and moats behind me.

Enter Megan, the princess's sister. "Our father has heard of your desire to leave," she said, pushing her voice a little. Sort of like she was corralling a group of camp kids.

Tyler touched my elbow. "Hey, that's your bud."

I opened my mouth and . . . Nothing. I just looked at him like an idiot. I *wanted* to point out that Megan is not my friend. Not really. But with that one little elbow touch he had managed the impossible—silencing Casey Smith.

"Father is sick with worry!" Megan exclaimed. "You must rid your mind of those wild dreams. They are nothing but dreams spun on gossamer lace." Her hands did this jaunty butterfly thing— I didn't know what to call it. Was she spinning lace or swatting a fly? Hard to say.

I joined in the applause as the curtain whooshed shut. Next on the program:

SKETCH NUMBER THREE:
Autumn: A Soliloquy by Jenna Randazzo.

Did Jenna show?

When the curtains opened on cue, I let out a sigh of relief.

Too soon.

"What's going on?" Tyler whispered to me. "Isn't a soliloquy just one person? Someone in drama needs help in the math department."

He was referring to the fact that there were

two kids on stage. Both wore robot costumes that sent beeps and blips through the audience. Neither of them was Jenna.

"They skipped to the final sketch." I crunched down on the end of my pen, checking the program:

SKETCH NUMBER FOUR:
Winter: Deep Freeze on Delta 9.

Some kind of sci-fi routine, best I could guess. But I was in a deep freeze of my own. Where was Jenna?

I slid to the edge of my seat, wishing I could split myself in two. One Casey to hang with Tyler. One to track down Jenna.

I had to go.

"See you later," I whispered to Tyler. "I've got to check something out."

He nodded as I left.

A nod. He didn't hate me. Whoopee!

It was easy to find Megan backstage. How could anyone *miss* her in that spiderweb of netting and sparkles? She and Toni stood in the wings, watching as Anna Zafrani strode onto the stage in green makeup, with pointy ears and gnarled green fingers as long as bread sticks. As

171

she spoke her first line, I saw her glance toward the wings where Ringo sat with a copy of the script, just out of sight of the audience.

"Jenna never showed?" I whispered.

Toni got a shot of the action on stage, then shook her head. "No, and I'm really starting to—"

"Shhh!" Someone on the crew waved us back.

I pulled Toni and Megan over to a quiet corner. "I have a bad feeling about this. We need to find Jenna. Now."

"I'm with you," Toni said, tugging her camera strap over her wild hair.

"Should we call the police?" Megan asked.

I swallowed hard, considering it. "What would we say? We *think* our friend's boyfriend is beating her up? We think she *might* be with him? Get real."

"I just can't believe she blew off the show!" Toni said, waving toward the stage. "What could be more important than this?"

"Whatever AJ wanted to do," I guessed. "Sixteen-year-old boys who beat on their girl-friends are kind of a foreign species to me. What do you guys think he'd be up to on a Thursday night?"

As soon as I looked at Toni, it hit me.

"The party," I said. "She must've gone . . ."

"Oh, man! Why didn't I think of that before?" Toni exclaimed, knocking her forehead with the palm of her hand.

"Shhh!" came another order from a crew member.

Megan looked clueless. "What party?"

"You remember the note Jenna slipped me yesterday? She wanted me to go with her to some party by some lake." Toni talked a mile a minute as she wrapped the strap around her camera.

"It's got to be at the lodge," I said. "The one by Crystal Lake."

I knew the place. I'd heard about stuff that went on there from my brother, Billy.

"I can't believe the lodge members are going to allow a bunch of teenagers to have a party," Megan said, drawing her brows together. "On a school night?"

"Get a grip, girl," Toni told Megan. "No one is allowing anything. Those kids are crashing the place."

If Megan's mouth had dropped open any wider, you could have used it as a steam shovel. "What? They can't!"

In that instant, I made a decision. "I'm going."

"You can't!" Megan shook her head so frantically, her netting shivered.

"I've got to." I was already digging my backpack and jacket out from under the mound of stuff in the corner.

"I'm with you," Toni agreed. "If she's with AJ, she's in danger."

"But . . . it'll be all older kids. Who knows what they're doing?" Megan looked back and forth between Toni and me. "You don't know that Jenna's there. And what about the show? We need photos. And a review."

Toni put the lens cap on her camera and paused. "Okay, girl's got a point. I already arranged with Mr. DeLucca to get photos of the cast after the show."

I pulled on my jacket. "I'm still going. I can get info for the review from Toni." I moved back toward the wings. "Ringo can go with me."

"No can do." Toni grabbed my arm to stop me. "He's running lines for Anna. She said she can't concentrate with anyone else."

"And naturally that's more important than finding Jenna," I muttered. "Fine. Then I'll go alone."

I was halfway to the stage door when someone yanked on my sleeve.

"I can't let you go, Casey."

It was Princess Megan, putting her royal foot down. "It's not safe. A sixth grader can't go to a party like that."

I didn't realize white gauze and sparkles could make such an effective roadblock. But hey, Casey Smith, Sensitive Reporter, can also kick butt as Casey Smith, Steamroller.

I crossed my arms over the front of my jacket. "I'm going."

"No," she said again. "Not alone."

Standoff. What could we do? Flip a coin? Arm wrestle? No time for that.

"Fine, Princess." I grabbed Megan's crown from the makeup table and handed it to her. "Then you're coming with me."

"What!" Megan pulled back. As if I were dragging her to a pit of acid.

"Jenna needs help. Now!" I said. "What if we don't go and something happens to her? Could you live with that?"

I could see the Good Girl–Bad Girl war going on inside Princess Perfect. "All right, I'll do it," she said at last. "Just let me go tell my parents that I have to stay late and clean up."

Megan tell a fib? I never thought I'd see the day.

Girls Join High Order of Buffalo Beaks

PICTURE IT. TWO eleven-year-old girls, heading out to an Unauthorized High School Party. Chasing down a friend whose older boyfriend beat her up.

Think we were in over our heads?

Megan had the good idea to call the town taxi service. Riding our bikes out to Crystal Lake after dark wasn't the smartest move. Besides, all that gauze would have gotten tangled in Megan's spokes.

The taxi came right away. It figured that we would wind up with a nosy taxi driver. She kept checking us out in the rearview mirror, asking questions.

"What's with the costume?" she asked as we drove away from the rows of houses onto a road lined with trees and fences. "It's a little early for Halloween."

"I'm an actress," Megan told her proudly.

I snorted. "And I'm Marie of Romania."

Megan swung toward me. "What's that supposed to mean?"

Before I could answer, our driver shot back: "Isn't it kind of late for you girls to be going out to the lake? That area is fairly isolated."

No kidding! I thought as we passed a gas station—the only sign of civilization for a mile.

"We're meeting my father at the lodge," Megan lied. Two fibs in one night. I practically coughed from disbelief.

I spotted a sign saying BAIT AND TACKLE, but the tiny wood-shingled hut was dark. Probably closed for the season. It seemed like we were driving for hours.

At last I could see lights glowing from the lodge. A string of cars lined the gravel road that led up to the gates.

"You can drop us here," I told the driver, who was eyeballing the pack of parked cars.

"I thought the season out here ended after Labor Day," she said. "This looks like a pretty big to-do."

"It's a meeting of the grand high order of, um,

Buffalo Beaks. I mean, Buffalo Elks," I said, making up my story as I went along. "Our dads are members."

The driver was not convinced. She leveled a serious look at Megan and me while we scraped together the money to pay the fare.

"Call me crazy, but I didn't know you could cross a buffalo with an elk," she said. "Stay out of trouble, girls. Okay?"

"Hmm? Oh, sure!" Smiling bravely, Megan handed over the cash, climbed out and slammed the door.

It wasn't until after the cab drove off that she dropped the cheerful-camper grin. Gravel crunching under her satin slippers, she strode toward me. "Buffalo Elks?" she snapped. "What were you thinking? Don't you ever watch the Discovery Channel?"

"Give me a break," I said. "Geez, Megan. It wasn't like I had any time to rehearse. Unlike *you*."

Megan's face got this pinched look.

TACTLESS REPORTER RUFFLES FEATHERS

"If you're talking about my performance tonight, well . . . take your best shot."

"You stunk," I told her. Don't ask me what happened to Casey Smith, Sensitive Reporter. "But you know what's weird? Even in theater, you play the Princess Reason. Is that art imitating life, or what?"

Megan stared down at the gravel as we started toward the lodge. "It was a last-minute thing," she said, all hurt. "I barely got to rehearse."

"Maybe acting just isn't for you," I told her. "You can't be perfect at *everything*."

Megan didn't answer.

I could see that the party had spilled outside the lodge. Silhouettes of people moved around two bonfires at the lake's edge.

"There really are a lot of kids here."

"Not really kids," Megan whispered. "It's guys. And teenage girls. Mostly guys, though."

Through the lodge windows I could see kids dancing. But most people were just hanging around. Laughter and music blasted through the trees. Teenage laughter. Teenage music.

We were out of our league. By several years.

"They're drinking beer!" Megan said, grabbing my sleeve.

The flames of the bonfires threw light onto a metal keg near the water. Kids were bunched around it. All of a sudden I felt very short. In the dim light I could read the expression on Megan's face. Fear.

"We'll be fine," I lied. "Nobody's going to care

that we're younger. They might not even notice."

"Oh, right," she said, picking at her gauzy skirt. "You're not the one dressed like a Sugarplum Fairy."

Imagine that. For once my jeans and sweatshirt beat Megan's outfit. "Don't stress. It'll be cool," I lied again.

Our feet crunched on the tiny rocks as we made our way past the line of cars. Aside from the distant music and voices, the night was quiet. But as we passed a blue Camaro, I heard something else.

"Someone's crying," I said.

That's when we saw her . . . Jenna.

She was huddled inside the blue car, sobbing as she cradled her right arm. I held my breath when I saw the swollen wrist, mottled with purple.

AJ had done it again.

And we had to make it stop. Now.

I opened the car door and slipped into the backseat. Jenna pulled back toward the door when she saw me. Just then, Megan slid into the driver's seat and pulled the door shut against the cold.

"AJ did that to you, didn't he?" I asked.

Jenna wiped the tears from her cheeks with the sleeve of her unhurt arm. "It's . . . not what it looks like," she said. "AJ's a really great guy. I . . . I fell this time. For real. AJ would never hurt me on purpose!"

"A great guy wouldn't hurt your arm, Jenna," Megan said gently. "Or give you a black eye."

Jenna just shook her head as new tears rolled down her cheeks. "Just get AJ for me, okay?"

"Why? So he can sprain your other wrist?" I asked. Okay, I still had to work on my sensitivity training. But couldn't Jenna see that this guy was going to keep hurting her?

Apparently not.

"I need him," she went on. "My arm really hurts. AJ will know what to do. He always does."

Her voice was so small and pitiful. I felt sorry for her. But there was no way I was going to look for that creep.

"We have to get you to a safe place," Megan said.

"There's a gas station just down the road," I remembered. "I saw it on the way here."

Jenna still didn't seem to get it. "Just let me talk to AJ," she sobbed.

"You don't need him," I said firmly. "We'll call my grandmother from the gas station. She'll take you to the hospital."

Jenna looked about as happy as a dog headed for the pound. But I guess she could see we meant business. Or maybe her arm hurt too much to fight us. Whatever the reason, she didn't argue when we pulled her out of the car and steered her toward the road.

Talk about slow going. A three-girl demonstration of a snail's pace.

At least she's going with us, I thought, shivering in the cool night air. Jenna would be safe. For now. If we could just figure out how to get our message through her thick skull!

We were about halfway to the gas station when I heard another distant moan. A dog? Coyote?

No.

Sirens.

Heading our way.

"The cops!" I motioned Megan and Jenna to the edge of the road. "The cab driver must have called them. I bet they're raiding the party! We've got to get out of here."

Megan nodded toward Jenna's injured arm. "But we can't run," she said.

Translation: Time to panic!

"Just act cool," I said. As if my heart wasn't pumping out a gazillion beats a second. "Maybe they won't notice us."

One look at Megan's dress, glowing like pixie dust in the headlights of the cruiser, and I knew how ridiculous that was.

The siren blared again, sending my heart jumping up to the roof of my mouth. I froze as the car pulled up beside us . . . then zoomed past.

You never saw three more relieved girls.

"Talk about lucky," I said when I could breathe again.

But I spoke too soon. A minute later, we were caught in the headlights of another police car.

This one pulled up beside us, lights flashing.

A voice boomed from the speaker:

"Stop right where you are, girls."

Wanna-be Princess
Wins Award

A ZILLION HEADLINES flashed through my mind.

ELEVEN-YEAR-OLD PARTY GIRLS BUSTED!

PRETEEN DELINQUENTS GET 20-TO-LIFE...

I mean, who knew what kind of stuff they had at that party? Definitely alcohol. Maybe even drugs.

As the doors of the police car creaked open, I saw Megan's blue eyes widen. If she'd been hooked up to a panic meter, it would be blipping off the charts.

PERKY PRINCESS WAILS:
"CASEY MADE ME DO IT!"

Megan looked as if she might burst into tears any second. Then . . . she changed. Suddenly, she seemed taller, more confident. Was that a *smile* I saw curving her lips? I felt as if I was watching one of those transforming toys make the switch to an alternate form.

"Good evening, officers," she said in a sugar-coated voice.

I blinked. Whoa. Transformation complete. The way Megan was looking at the two officers who walked toward us, you would think they had come to hand out holiday gifts. Not to bust us.

"Boy, are we glad to see you!" Megan gushed.

WANNA-BE PRINCESS GOES OFF DEEP END

Or was this the performance of a lifetime? Clearing the frogs out of my throat, I added, "Um, yeah! We sure are."

The words fell like lead balloons. Scratch acting from my list of lifetime ambitions.

Jenna kept quiet. I noticed she had tucked her injured wrist into her jacket pocket. Her face was filled with pain. And confusion. And fear.

One officer, a tall guy with dark hair, flipped open his police pad and angled a dubious glance at us. "What are you ladies up to tonight? It's kind of late to be out here all by yourselves."

"You wouldn't happen to be coming from the lodge, would you?" added his partner, a stocky guy with dark brown skin and a wide mouth.

Megan swooshed her skirt around and said in a surprised tone, "The lodge? Why would we go there?" Her face was a halo of innocence. "Doesn't it close after Labor Day?"

I listened for the slightest hint of stiffness. The smallest nervous tic. Nothing.

But those cops looked as if they'd seen their share of performances. "It's supposed to be closed," said the stocky cop, crossing his arms over the front of his uniform. "Which brings us back to our original question: What are you doing out here?"

Megan didn't miss a beat. "We wouldn't even *be* here except that my mom forgot to pick us up. She's always forgetting things! We waited and waited at the school. I was in the show there," she said. "Did you hear about it? It's called *Collages*. Actually, I had a starring role. As a princess. But you probably could have guessed that, huh?" Megan plucked at her gauzy skirt as her laugh twittered into the still night.

"Sweetheart," one of the cops said, "you're a long way from Trumbull."

"That's what I was saying," Megan went on.

I was in shock. That laughter. The way she was rambling on. It seemed totally natural. Was this really Megan? Miss Rules and Regulations? Lying through her perfectly aligned teeth? To the *police*?

And you know what? She actually had them listening. They started to lose their lock-'em-up frowns. The tall one even smiled as he tried to steer Megan back to the point yet again: what we were doing out by the lake after dark.

"Oh! Right," Megan said, giggling. "When my mom didn't show, we got a ride out to Jenna's house." She clapped a hand on Jenna's shoulder. Jenna tried to rearrange her face so it looked like she knew what was happening. "Only Jenna's parents weren't home. *And* she forgot her keys! Is that bad luck or what?"

Megan bit her lip, pouring on just the right amount of concern. "It was too cold to wait around outside the house. So we started walking to the gas station. We were going to call *her* mom," she said, pointing to me. "But I guess we took a wrong turn out here in the boondocks. It's so dark and the road twists around so much and . . . we got so incredibly lost."

I could practically hear the soundtrack swell in the background. Talk about a performance. This was a thousand times better than the one Megan had pulled off onstage.

But the question was, did the cops buy it?

"Girls, get in the back of the squad car, please."

Uh-oh. We really were busted.

But Megan was a true professional. She went right into a You're-My-Hero routine as a last try at freedom.

I hate to admit this, but I will: She was awesome. Not that it mattered. The stocky cop opened the back door and held out a hand. "Girls? In the car. Now."

I turned to Jenna. I don't know what I expected. Relief? Thanks? But she just stood there, holding her arm. Her blond hair hung limply around her face. Her red-rimmed eyes were a total blank. I couldn't begin to guess what was going through her mind.

"Okay," the tall cop said as we piled in. "We need to locate a parent who can vouch for you."

"My grandmother!" I piped up. "She can vouch for all of us. And she's home right now." I gave them the address, then sank back in relief. We weren't busted. Well, when Gram heard what happened, some punishment might be in order.

She might actually make me clean my room. That's definitely cruel and unusual.

* * *

"Someone should give serious consideration to the design of hospital emergency rooms," I said, an hour later.

Gram had left Jenna, Megan and me in the waiting room of Hawthorne Memorial Hospital while she went to find a phone to call Jenna's dad. Not that I was preoccupied with the decor or anything. But Jenna had been about as talkative as a block of wood. Can you blame me for babbling?

I nodded at the green linoleum floor, the rows of chairs, the grim insurance notices posted next to the nurses' station. "This place doesn't exactly encourage healing. If the signs don't bore you to death, the plastic pod chairs will give you a backache."

I slid the soles of my purple Converses along the linoleum and glanced at Jenna. Nothing.

Megan shrugged and shifted in her chair. She was getting a lot of looks from other people waiting to see a doctor. One kid asked her if she was a ballerina.

"So . . ." Megan turned to look at Jenna. "You know we have to tell the doctor about AJ. And your dad."

Miss Rules and Regulations was back. But this time I was on her side.

Jenna's eyes flashed moodily. "AJ is my boyfriend," she said. "He *loves* me!"

189

I remembered what I read about teenage relationship abuse. About how victims confused violence for affection. Jenna was just thirteen. How much dating experience could she have had?

"Is AJ the first guy you've gone out with?" I asked her.

Jenna nodded, her eyes misting. "Yeah. Before that . . . well, I guess I always felt kind of insecure around guys, you know?"

"You?" Megan shot a surprised look at Jenna. "But you're so outgoing and funny."

Jenna shrugged, slumping lower in her chair. "He's my first real boyfriend. I can't lose him."

I wanted to yell: *"But you're in the eighth grade! You've got years and years of boyfriends ahead!"* The old me would have, but not Casey Smith, Sensitive Reporter.

"I never thought any guy would want to get to know what I was *really* like," Jenna went on. "Then I met AJ. He was so cute and so cool! When he started flirting with me . . ." She smiled. "He made me feel special. It was like being in a movie."

"Except this one didn't have a very happy ending, did it?" I asked, even though it really wasn't a question.

Jenna didn't give any sign that she'd heard me. "We spent the summer hanging out. We'd talk for hours. He's a really sweet guy. He said he never wanted me to leave his side."

The guy had sent her to the ER. How could she call him sweet?

But again, I bit my tongue. Casey Smith, Quiet Listener. Plus this was really serious. Flip wouldn't help Jenna.

"When did he start to hurt you?" Megan asked.

Jenna frowned. "I'm not sure. He just lost his temper at first. You know, about little things. Like if he called and I didn't call him back right away. Or if I spilled something in his car. The first time he hit me . . ." Her head sank down against her chest for a moment. "I was sure it was a fluke. I never thought it would happen again."

"And the second time?" I asked.

"I was late meeting him. It was my fault," Jenna said quickly.

ABUSED GIRL STUNS REPORTERS WITH EXCUSES

I guess she read the shock in our faces.

"You think I'm crazy to love AJ," she said, blinking back tears. "But I do."

I remembered what Kid Helpers said about how victims will defend their abusers. Jenna was a classic case. "What about your dad?" I asked. "Why didn't you tell him when AJ started to hurt you?"

"So he could ground me forever?" Jenna said, blowing out an angry breath. "Dad hates AJ."

Gee, I wonder why, I thought.

"It's hard enough sneaking out to see him now," Jenna crossed her arms over her chest, tapping her boot against the floor. "Can you imagine what my dad would do if he knew? He'd go wild. He'd probably call the police."

I couldn't believe what I was hearing. "You let Toni and me believe your dad was hurting you. What if we had reported *that* to the police?"

"It's not like I had a big plan to mislead you," Jenna said. "But when I saw that you guys assumed it was my father . . ." She shrugged. "What could I do? If I told you the truth, I knew I'd get AJ in trouble. I'd lose him."

Megan's skirt rustled as she leaned forward. "And that would be a *bad* thing?" she asked.

"AJ and I can work this out," Jenna insisted. "He's been going through some bad stuff, that's all. He never means to hurt me."

The girl was seriously confused. Totally out of touch with reality.

"AJ's not going through some phase," Megan said. "Casey and I have both talked to people with experience in abuse. Jenna, AJ won't change unless he gets professional help."

"You can't change him, Jenna," I added.

"You've got to stop taking the blame. Start worrying about yourself."

Curling up, Jenna pulled up her knees and wrapped her arms around them.

"Jenna Randazzo?" An attendant waved to us from the nurses' station. "Doctor Ramos can see you now."

You never saw anyone make such a quick getaway. As Jenna disappeared down the hall behind the nurse, Megan sighed and crossed her legs. Her satin slippers were torn and dirty. Kind of like our morale.

"You think we got through to her?" she asked.

"No," I said. "But at least it's not a secret anymore. Something has to happen now. Maybe things will get better."

Megan shrugged. "Maybe."

Boy Cheers: "Rah-Rah, Sis-Boom Blast-Off!"

FRIDAY MORNING CAME too soon.

After a late night of hospitals and phone calls and e-mails, I could have stayed glued to my pillow until way past my normal get-up-and-go time. School tends to clip the edges of the envelope. But even though Gram said I could sleep in, I couldn't slack off.

We had a newspaper to get out.

"I need your help with the rest of my write-up on *Collages*, guys," I said to Toni and Ringo as I plodded into the newsroom. Dalmatian Station was covered with photos from the performances. "I hope you have lots of pics from the last sketch."

"Toni told me about what happened with Jenna," Ringo said.

While Megan and I had been waiting at the hospital, we'd done this phone-chain, e-mail thing to get the word on Jenna out to the staff. And to Griffin.

"You think she's gonna be okay?" Ringo asked.

REPORTER FAILS TO SAVE FELLOW STUDENT

"Maybe," I said.

There was that word again. Like *maybe* we'd find a cure for cancer. And *maybe* we'd stop blasting polluted holes in the ozone layer. I was officially overwhelmed.

Shaking myself, I opened my journal to a fresh page. "So, what happened after I left?"

"Okay, Picture it. Anna Zafrani decked out in alien slime and icicles." Toni jabbed a sparkly red fingernail at one of the shots on the spotted table. "The sole survivor of a starship civilization that's been enslaved by Delta Nine's new Robo-Cop Squad. At least that's what the sleazoid robo-trash want her to believe. You should have seen Anna sneaking past the enemy to get to the Deep Freeze—this forbidden zone where she's sure there are more of her kind. I'm telling you, she was so hot, she scorched the ice to boiling water."

"You've got a real style, Toni," I said, as I scribbled down notes. "How come you never write any articles?"

Toni drew herself up and gave me The Look. "Get real, girl. I do pictures, not words. You know that. Or, you would, if you took your brains out of your backpack." She flipped her hair at me, as if I had insulted her.

Never try to compliment a tiger.

"Guys! We're in trouble!" Megan ran into the room with Gary behind her.

"No kidding." Ringo gave Megan the once-over. "Your socks are earth tone, and your headband is more of an amber. A definite fashion don't."

I don't think Megan even heard him. She hurried over to one of the computers and fumbled through the disks. "Gary says the layout for page one is really light. We need something to replace Casey's story on abuse."

GIRL REPORTER FAILS

I had made a guess. Jumped to a humongous conclusion about Jenna's father and typed it up in black and white. Staked my reputation as a reporter on a theory without enough evidence to back it up.

I can tell you one thing. I will never do that again.

Megan pulled my story on I KNOW HE CARES from her backpack and smoothed the crumpled pages. "Maybe there's a way to salvage this. . . ."

Not exactly a huge vote of confidence.

"So you wanna see my cube?" Ringo asked. He came over to Megan holding a piece of paper.

"We already chose two cartoons," Megan said. "I don't want to overload—"

"Hey," I cut in, staring at the paper in Ringo's hand. "These are words. Not cartoons."

Megan straightened up to get a better look. "You wrote a story?"

Ringo handed over the page, grinning. "More sides of the cube."

Megan and I bent over the story. We were so curious, we practically devoured it:

CONFESSIONS OF A BOY CHEERLEADER
    Hey. Most of you know me as the kid who draws the dude Simon. I'm also a new cheerleader. And a guy.
    Maybe you've heard about it? It's been going around school that some weird girly-guy is on the cheer squad. And people are laughing.
At me.

I thought the hardest part would
be walking out on that field and
turning triple cartwheels with
the squad. Pass the reality serum!
The thing that takes real guts is
walking down the halls at school
and facing the salty 'tudes who
look at me and see a strange softee
who's afraid to play football.

News flash: Playing sports no
more makes you a dude than eating
spaghetti makes you Italian.

I'm a guy, thank you very much.
I just happen to be a guy who
digs cheerleading because I'm
into gymnastics. Did you know the
average cheerleader needs to know
how to do a back handspring *and* a
back flip? When was the last time
you did one lousy cartwheel?
Second grade?

Some kids think school spirit
is cheesy. I think it's cool like
a cube. You know how most people
put things in boxes? Neat and
nifty places to stereotype people
so that they can understand them.
Then they tease the boxed dude for

his choices, even though they put
him in that box.

I don't do boxes. I say "Right
on!" to you for whatever you do
because I put things in my head's
cube—a cube where everyone has
lots of different sides. Different
faces. Different dimensions.

If you still think being dudely
is about pushing guys around, or
worse, bulldozing girls around,
then I just don't know what to do
with you. I think it's cool if
you're a football player or you're
an actress, or science buff, or a
girl reporter, or *whatever* you do.

I won't ever box you up. You're
cube-a-licious!

So here's my righteous idea:
You groove on your own vibe. I'll
groove on mine. If we could do
that, school would RAWK!

    Peace out,
    Ringo

When I looked up, Ringo was standing there
with his trademark goofy smile. "Well?"

"Ringo, I didn't know you were so bummed

about all this," I admitted. "I guess I've been so wrapped up in my own stuff that I haven't been listening to you that much."

Ringo's eyebrows shot up. "That much?"

"Ditto from me," Gary added. Talk about choking on an apology. "Not that I think cheerleading is cool or anything. But I get why you want to do it, dude."

"You make a great point, Ringo. Cheerleading isn't male or female," Megan said, pointing at the article with a glittery pencil. "It's our perception that paints it that way."

Thank you, Yoda.

But Megan was right. Again. Either you solve a problem or you make it worse. I was so busy solving Jenna's problem and the problem of scoring a front-page story that I didn't read between the lines with Ringo. I felt bad.

"Ringo," I said, Sensitive Reporter in full swing. "I'm really sorry I teased you. Can you forgive me?"

Ringo held out his hands like a TV evangelist. "Forgive. Forget. And I'll expect you to supply me with nachos at every game. A guy needs his cheering fuel."

Megan cut into our love-fest. "This is super, Ringo," she said. "We can run it with your Simon cartoons on page five."

Megan put Ringo's story on top of her clipboard. Then she clapped her perfect hands and said, "Let's get down to business, guys. We've got some stories to finish."

She didn't need the costume. Princess Megan was back on her throne.

We manned the PCs and got back to work. But before I got back to my *Collages* story, I sneaked a look at my e-mail. Yes! Griffin had answered my message from late last night.

To: Wordpainter
From: Thebeast
Re: TOAST (Totally Off Advice Sinks Trumbull)
Nice story. I especially like the part about the princess and the cop. Sounds like Megan has some hidden acting talent. I smell a story. Or is that bacon from downstairs? Gotta run. Breakfast.

P.S. Don't feel too bad about Jenna. Maybe you helped her to start turning things around. . . .

Front-Page Story
Bites the Dust!

I SENT OFF a quick response to Griffin. Then I went back to work on *Real News*. Megan was right about one thing. With all that had been going on, we were behind.

Way behind.

At least we were getting real experience dealing with deadline insanity. All of us switched into crisis-management mode. Toni fed me details I needed for my write-up of *Collages*. Megan went to work editing Gary's story on the Deergrass-Trumbull football game. Gary wrote a blurb to go with Ringo's cheerleading editorial. Ringo worked on photo captions and laid out space for the photos of *Collages* that he and Toni had picked out.

Somehow I finished my review in record time.

But even after I handed it over to Megan for editing, something kept nagging at me.

REPORTER FALLS SHORT OF EXPECTATIONS

I only had one story for this edition. My review of *Collages*. Not exactly a heavyweight piece of reporting.

The big story of the moment had slipped through my fingers . . .

Or had it?

I kept thinking about Jenna. A kid right here at Trumbull who was the victim of abuse. Relationship abuse. Other kids could learn a lot from her story. I really wanted to write it up. My motives were pure. Sort of.

But . . . would Jenna let me?

I checked my watch. The deadline loomed. I didn't even know whether Jenna was in school, much less whether she would talk to me. Grabbing my journal, I ran for the door.

"Where are you going?" Megan called out. I didn't have to see the frown. I could hear it in her voice. "We still have to format your article and . . ."

"I'll be back as soon as I can," I said over my shoulder. "I just have to see if I can find . . ."

My voice trailed off when I spotted her outside the doorway. "Jenna," I said, stopping short.

Her arm was in a sling. The bruise around her eye was still visible, though fading. But what really came through was the smoldering anger. It heated up her whole body. And it was aimed right at me.

"Why did you have to butt into my business?" she asked, glaring at me.

"I wanted to help," I said. Talk about gratitude.

"We all did," Toni spoke up from behind me.

Jenna took a step into the newsroom. "Oh, yeah? Well, thanks to all your *help*, my father called the police. He's pressing charges against AJ, and he's making me get counseling," she snapped. "Thanks to you, my life is ruined!"

"Take a look in the mirror, Jenna," I said, trying to keep my own temper in check. "Last week, it was a black eye. This week, a sprained arm. What's it going to be next week? And the week after?"

Jenna shook her head bitterly back and forth. "You don't get it, do you? AJ and I would still be together if it weren't for you."

Something was seriously wrong with this picture. I decided to try a different approach.

"Dating violence happens more than you would think," I said. "Don't you want to do something to get the truth to other kids? To let them know they're not alone? That they can get help, too?"

"What do AJ and I have to do with other kids?" Jenna asked. "What are you talking about?"

I took a deep breath, gripping my journal more tightly. "A story," I said. "I'll work with you. Tell your side of the story."

Her eyes burned into me. If looks could really kill, I would be a dead preteen.

Then she snapped.

"Are you out of your mind! Do you know how furious my father was when the doctor told him what was going on? I'm grounded. Probably forever, thanks to you. And you have the nerve to ask me to help you write a story?"

A simple no would have sufficed. But Jenna stood there steaming. As if she were waiting for me to apologize and slap together a happy ending for her.

What did I expect? That she would thank me, Casey Smith, Sensitive Reporter, for my incredible restraint? I wanted that story. I *really* wanted it. But she was too confused. Too angry. I had to let it go. "Sorry," I said.

Jenna left the room.

Taking my story with her.

I stood there staring after her.

"Casey?" Megan spoke up.

She was right next to me. Was that sympathy I saw in her eyes?

It was enough to make me gag.

"You did the right thing, you know," Megan said.

"What?" I turned around and slammed my journal down on Dalmation Station. "Losing a huge story? Knocking myself senseless trying to help someone who just resents me for it?"

Megan shook her head. "I know how much you wanted that story. But you did everything you could for Jenna. She's the real victim here, even if she is kind of angry with you right now."

"Kind of?" Gary put in.

"The point is, Casey didn't take advantage of her," Megan said. "I think that shows a lot of sensitivity."

I groaned. There was that "S" word again.

GIRL REPORTER LOSES EDGE

"Journalists aren't supposed to be sensitive," I retorted. "If a reporter backs off a story because she's afraid of hurting someone's feelings . . ." I couldn't even finish my sentence. "Case closed."

"Maybe not," Toni said.

Her face was thoughtful as she twirled her wild orange hair around one finger.

"What are you talking about?" I asked.

"You could talk to an observer," Toni said.

"Someone on the fringes, someone whose friend was being abused right under her nose. Someone who feels guilty that she wasn't wise to that pond-scum lizard boyfriend. Without, of course, naming names. You know . . . 'Sources say' kind of stuff . . ."

A huge grin spread across my face as the story took shape in my mind. I'd never expected Toni to offer to spill her guts. I guess she wanted the story to get out there, too. "Sounds good to me."

Gary, Megan and Ringo stopped working to look up.

"We'll have to carve out room on page one," Gary pointed out. "That means totally changing the layout."

"We can do that," said Ringo.

Megan nodded, making new notations on her clipboard. "I like it. I like it a lot."

"Okay then." I picked up a pencil, opened my journal and turned to Toni. "Start talking, girl."

My Word
by Linda Ellerbee

MY NAME IS LINDA ELLERBEE. I'm a journalist.
Sometimes, when covering a story, I have secret
sources, people who tell me things, but don't,
for one reason or another, want their identities
revealed. This can be a good thing. For instance,
when I was covering the United States Congress,
occasionally a senator would tell me exactly how
the vote was going to go on a certain piece of
legislation—before anyone else knew. A thing like
that allowed me to go on the air (I worked for
NBC News then) and tell everybody what I had
found out—and beat the competition!

But often the decisions weren't so simple.
Once in a while I would find out something that
made me think I ought to NOT go on the air and
tell it. Sometimes I couldn't be sure: Was it real
news, or just gossip? Was it my job to decide?

We all face choices like this in one way or
another throughout our lives. Casey and Megan
both faced similar choices in this book. Is it ever
okay to "tell" on a friend? Are there times when

revealing a secret is the best thing to do, and if so, whom do you tell?

I wish I could say there are easy answers to questions like this. Casey always likes a simple answer and so do I, but even Casey is coming to understand that simple is not the same as easy. And that choices have consequences.

Maybe that's why Casey and I both mistrust advice columns. They often try to turn a gray world into strictly black and white. Only *one* right. Only *one* wrong. Only *one* answer to a question, if you please (and don't color outside the lines, kid).

Bah.

Life is messy. It just is. And that doesn't start when you grow up. It's messy when you're eleven. You're a kid—and you like being a kid— but a more real, and possibly more complicated world sits outside your room. Do you invite it in? Open the door and run headlong into a reality that might not be so pretty? Or do you shut your door and your eyes and keep the door locked?

You tell me. I think it's pretty tough to be your age.

And then there's the boy thing.

At eleven, I was, in my mind, basically dorky. Brown eyes, brown hair, brown freckles. A little sloppy about my appearance. A big mouth that regularly got me in trouble (sound familiar?). And a habit of telling boys exactly what I thought about them. Most of them, I remember, had bumps and sweaty palms, which I always pointed out to them, but there were a few guys. . . .

The thing was, part of me wanted to stay a kid forever, to stop the rush of time . . . but another part of me wanted to grow up just as fast as I could. That part of me had a huge crush on an older boy. Not only was he older, he had a little bit of a bad rep. He was, everybody said, "dangerous." I found that extremely attractive. There's something about "bad" boys, y'know?

Once he asked me to go for a ride with him in his car. (He was fifteen and when I grew up, in Texas, we got our driving licenses when we were fourteen! Can you believe it?) I went, without exactly telling my mother, who, I assure you, would not have approved. We drove to the beach, where Mr. Shaggy-Hair-Falling-Into-His-Slightly-Sleepy-Eyes-But-Oh-What-a-Grin assumed that certain things might happen. He kissed me. It was my first kiss. (I do not count the time Johnny Hansen tried to kiss me when I was rounding third base back in the first grade; besides, I punched him out for his efforts.) This was different, and while it wasn't exactly unpleasant, it was a little scary. Suddenly I wanted to go back, and not just go back home. I wanted to go back to being a kid, someone who didn't have to make these kinds of choices.

At that moment, I wanted to never grow up.

I didn't tell him *that*. Instead I behaved in a perfectly grown-up, rational, sensible way. I burst into tears. He took me home *very* fast.

Now I'll never know what he intended to happen that afternoon, or how "dangerous" he really was. But this I do know: I had the right to say no. And so do you. I had the right to protect myself. And so do you. My method may have been clumsy, but my decision was not.

I never went off with this older guy in his car again. I chose to wait, to let time slow down a little, to keep on being a kid for a bit longer. But did I absolutely stop thinking this guy was cute in his bad-boy way?

Get real.

FROM

Girl Reporter Snags Crush!

MY NAME IS Casey Smith, and I am the only sane person in my entire school.

It started this morning. It seemed like any other Thursday. I pulled on my favorite pair of perfectly broken-in blue jeans, a white T-shirt, and my red Converse high-tops. Then I lugged my backpack onto my shoulder and headed out the door. Believe me, I wasn't expecting this Thursday to be anything out of the ordinary.

I mean, Trumbull Middle School isn't exactly the home of all things strange but true. As far as schools go, it's your standard mixture of beige walls and brown lockers. And Abbington, the supersleepy town where I live in the Berkshire Mountains in western Massachusetts, makes everything seem so uneventful. They should rename this place Dullsville. Or Boringland.

Not exactly a big humming city.

Actually, it's not even a small humming city.

At least I've got the school newspaper, *Real News*, to keep me busy. It's true that I have to keep my reporter's radar on overdrive to find anything juicy, but I do manage to write up some hard-hitting stories when it really counts.

Most of the time.

There has been the occasional issue where my name didn't appear on the front page. But it wasn't my fault. I blame those practically unreadable issues on our editor in chief, Megan O'Connor, better known as the Princess of Pink, or the Sugarplum Fairy, or (fill in your favorite gooey word here). She and I have very different ideas about what makes good news.

My ideas: environmental pollution, child abuse, crooked community leaders. *Real* news. News that matters. Megan's ideas: school plays, parades, cheerleading tryouts.

With that mentality, why not just write about this week's beefaroni special in the school cafeteria?

PARENTS PROTEST BARFARONI HOT LUNCH!
Hundreds of Kids Hurl Through Night Following Trumbull Meal!

Do I sound like I'm on my reporter's soapbox? It happens. Megan gets under my freckled skin like no one else.

But more on Megan later. As I said, it started out a normal morning. I walked the last few blocks to school, passing more and more kids. Just like always.

But they were acting strange.

Take Gary Williams, for example. Gary's the sports reporter for *Real News*. He's a jock, fine, but he also has a pretty sharp brain. Usually.

But today, Gary was low on gray matter. Actually, pink matter was flying over his head. He was holding up a neon-purple notebook, sassing some girl. His baby dreadlocks swayed, and his brown lips were curved in a goofy grin. Then he took off running.

"Coming through!" Gary hollered, nearly knocking me out of my hightops. He bolted past me and across the school lawn. That's when I noticed the pink flamingos on his notebook. Correction: it was definitely not his notebook.